# Imagine all the People
## Andrien Beck
**Copyright 2025**

## Chapter 1:

There was a time when I thought every action, every moment, was a wild card. None of that *predetermined*, ordained by a higher power nonsense. Instances of beauty and the unfortunate moments of disaster playing out before me in real time were nothing more than the luck of the draw. The strength of this ideology buried its claws deep into my neck at a young age. You know, I once watched a person burn at the side of the road?

I slowed my car to a modest thirty-five miles an hour and had enough respect to only stare out the corner of my eyes as I passed the wreckage. The bright red paint of the fire truck harmonized with the orange flames and black smoke pluming from the twisted vehicle. Men raced around the wreckage, pulling on thick brown hoses with copper necks. The water evaporated against the charred steel, hissing through the tightly sealed window of my Hyundai Elantra. I squeezed the steering wheel as I rolled past the scene, arching my eyes against the side of their sockets. My breath hitched when the passenger's visage peered from behind a curtain of black smoke. The melting flesh writhed like a multitude of worms in a bucket. Its mouth, locked in a scream, showing its teeth like a rabid dog. The shoulders slumped behind the burning seatbelt. The strap pressed the corpse to the seat in a vice of death.

Behind the wreckage, a looming billboard cut through the rising smoke and flames. A police officer with the brim of his hat covering his eyes stared down with his finger pointed accusingly at the reader. Huge white letters in sharp Sans-Serif font read *Click It or Ticket*. The irony was disconcerting. I slid my hand down the side of my body in a slow arch, unhitching my belt, letting it slide across my waist as I stared at the melting corpse. Early this morning, that poor soul was brushing his or her teeth. Maybe they were late for work and rushed to make their cup of coffee. They run their hand over their spouse's shoulder, no need to be too affectionate. They could make up for that later. Bending to kiss the children on their foreheads, yelling their love as they exit into the morning grind. Now, they melt into the disintegrating fabric of their overpriced car.

All of this is a wild card. Luck of the draw. I mean, imagine an entity trying to calculate and maintain order to all this chaos. Impossible. A few years back, I walked into a quicky mart and stood in line behind a middle-aged woman with bright pink hair and facial piercings. She purchased a pack of cigarettes and a scratch-off lottery ticket. For whatever reason, I also bought a scratch-off ticket. It's not like it was my first time, but it was rare. I sat in the parking lot, the silhouettes of strangers ebbing in my peripheral, as I pinched the dime between my thumb and forefinger. I won three hundred dollars that morning. Who could take the time to plan that? If that woman had been ten seconds later, she would have won it. Wild card, that's all this is. The question is, who shuffles the deck? This thought process still insinuated that there is a control element. Something that shuffles. Maybe someone. Without a doubt, if it's someone, that someone could cheat. I have a theory about all of this, but maybe we will get to that later.

For the meantime, I need a starting point on how my current situation came to fruition. What kind of wild card does a man deserve to draw that explains the choice or the appointed obligation from the Shuffler, to bludgeon strangers to death? That's a hell of a wild card, right? I am getting ahead of myself. Let me start with an appropriate part in my timeline. We will start on Monday, March 25th, 2024, the morning I woke up and found a dead body sitting in my living room watching The Weather Channel. That's as good a point as any. We can go back, if we have time, to discuss anything that needs cleared up, like my Shuffler theory. I woke up that morning needing to piss so hard my stomach hurt. I looked at the clock and rolled my eyes.

### March 25th, 2024, 5:45 am.

The sleep crust grips my eyelids closed as my mouth stretches wide, letting out an invisible scream. I was unaware of the ungodly time burning neon red across my cheap brushed steel Walmart alarm clock. I prefer my old school 80s Emerson shit brown model, but, somewhere in my multitude of relocation, it mysteriously disappeared. My wrist bone scrapes the crust away as the wailing high-pitched cry becomes a full-frontal assault on my senses. Moaning has yet to relinquish any agony, but it is my go-to. I catapult my open hand, using the force of my shoulder like a trebuchet, blindly targeting to sound. I have done this enough to know the exact location of the screamer. The sharp ping of pain usually rides up my forearm as the clock topples to the floor in defeat. You can imagine my confusion when my hand collided with the foe, toppling the assailant to the floor and swung, to dangle off the edge of the bed, sans pain.

Sans…pain. You got that, right? Just making sure you are paying attention.

I know this detail seems undramatic, but it is the apex of my current situation, and how I ended up stuffed under my bed with a hole in my chest. If I had stayed under the sheets that morning, it wouldn't have mattered. Lady Luck had played her hand. That dead body in my living room would be there regardless of the exact time I rose from slumber.

I swung my feet over the side of the bed and rubbed my wrist as I stared at the clock, now silent, on my bedroom floor. The fake wood felt cool against the bottom of my feet as I shifted my weight and stood, holding my piss in as the razors of light from the blinds cut into my back. Sheryl Crow fills the voids of my mind. The melody from "The First Cut is The Deepest" swells, making my head feel fuzzy. Associating music with a physical feeling has been something that I have been doing since I was a child. I imagine it is a comfort response. When I think back to when this behavior started, I cannot pinpoint the exact moment with certainty. But I stick strong to this memory.

The age of consent when I was a child was somewhere between fifteen and eighteen. None of my friends knew the exact and final range. Consent was a subject concerning sex and promiscuity in its legal form. I am not talking about that. There are other forms of consent that go unnoticed or ignored. Maybe it is for the sake of normality. A way for the educators to stick to what they know. As adults, they know about sex. There are exceptions, like Mr. Brummel. I don't think he had ever seen a set of naked tits that wasn't in a photographic medium. I am not talking about that kind of consent.

I came across the squirrel on my way home from school, missing the bus, fucking around with my friends. Instead of calling my mom, I walked home. I probably wouldn't have noticed the body if it weren't for its tail writhing in jerky movements above its backside. As I approached the middle of the road, I vaguely looked for oncoming traffic. Beady black eyes stared vacantly through me toward the sun. Its flattened abdomen pressed against the asphalt, turning the cracked grey around its form into a deep smooth crimson. As much as I wanted to walk away, I couldn't. It would have been far easier to move along, go home and make a snack before sneaking into the basement family room to play Defender. The critter looked into my eyes and lowered its tail into the intestines that were protruding from its backside. My throat sank into my stomach as my heart raced. It gave me consent to do what was necessary. Whether I wanted to or not was something different. That was something only I could accept. Finding a large stone in the ditch, I returned, holding it above my head like a gladiator. The sun warmed my neck as my arms trembled above my head. I closed my eyes and took a deep breath. "Sunshine on my Shoulders" by John Denver, filled the void behind my eyes as I drove the rock down. I beat my high score on Defender that afternoon.

Leaving the clock on the floor, I made my way to the bathroom. There was a solid ritual of urinating and then caffeine that needed to take place before anything else. Something important to note is that I have rituals. I am pretty sure this is the case with most people, but we all think ours is a unique happening, don't we? Well, mine are, so. Before I go to bed, I must shut off all lights and electronics, including my cell phone. The only exception, of course, is the alarm clock in my bedroom. So, you must imagine again my surprise when I recognized the voice of meteorologist Kathleen Kempt snaking from my living room. I will admit that I watch her more for her outfits and slim figure than I do the local forecast. I slowed my pace and crept to the end of the hallway, peering with one eye. Two things struck me. One, as a tall, thin woman with olive skin and platinum blonde hair, one must, in my opinion, stay away from plum colors. I forgive her again, but lately, it's been an ongoing trend, and I am questioning my obsession with this woman. Kathleen points to the upper right-hand corner of the screen and reports that although we are expecting rain, it will still be in the seventies throughout the day. Two, there's a stranger sitting on my couch watching The Weather Channel.

* * * *

My lower back ached as I emptied my bladder. I focused my attention on the bubbles that formed around the outer perimeter of the toilet bowl and tried to make sense of the stranger watching The Weather Channel. Who was sitting in my living room? How the hell did he get into my apartment, and did he like Kathleen's plum choice? I don't know what bothers me more. The lack of concern that the person in my living room may intend to do harm, or that he may or may not like the color of Kathleen's blouse. Before you ask, I could tell it was a "*he*". It was the broad shoulders and tight hair, and of course the beard. It makes no difference because anyone…anyone can inflict harm. People who have experienced similar situations have reported feeling their personal space had become invaded. I didn't feel that way. I do not understand why my personal space seemed fine. Until I approached him. All I knew was that I needed to find out how and why he was sitting on my couch watching Kathleen Kempt report on our local weather. I washed my hands and headed back out towards the living room. Again, I was unaware of the ease of my emotions until I approached the stranger. After saying hello more than I was comfortable, I poked his shoulder. He slumped forward, bouncing his head off my coffee table before collapsing to the floor. It was then that I realized my ease in the situation. He was dead. Dead people have a way of making an environment feel less threatening. I learned that along the way somehow.

I turned down the volume of the television and stared at his back for the better part of a half hour. I ran through several imaginary situations of how he could have entered my apartment and dispelled every instance by checking doors and windows. Checking him for bleeding, I felt no reason to move him and went about my morning, drinking coffee and debating on calling the police. The reality of calling the authorities had several of its own problems. They may think I had killed the stranger being the number one issue. My former explanation presumed the pretense of guilt. It was difficult cooking breakfast, but I managed to down two eggs and toast as I tried to work out what exactly I would need to do to get rid of the body. I gave up on how and why and focused on *"what now?"*. I am not gonna spend too much time on what I did the rest of the day. What I will do is tell you how I got rid of him.

Around seven o'clock every day, the building seemed to quiet down. Most of the tenants were home feeding their families or doing whatever strangers do. I had wrapped up the man's body in a bedsheet. Using another sheet, which I cut into strips, I tied the body around the ankles, midsection, and head. He looked like a mummy from the classic fifties movies I used to watch with my pa-pop.

Voices echoed through the hallways from behind closed doors as I dragged him to the garbage room. Once again, luck had played a major part, as not one person had come into the hallway as I made my way down. He didn't weigh an awful lot, and for that I was thankful, but my heart was beating so hard I thought I might pass out. With a bit of struggle, I leaned his top half into the garbage chute, which was larger than I remember, and slid his body in. I listened to a loud thump rattle from the depths of the shoot. Returning to my apartment, I flopped onto the couch where the stranger once sat and closed my eyes, spent. It wasn't until the next morning that I found another stranger lying on my kitchen floor. It is also the defining moment when my current predicament presented itself. I realized I was dead.

## Chapter 2:

My name is Thane Mortimer. Born in 1973. The only child of Kieth and Allison Mortimer. My father, Kieth, grew up somewhere in Kentucky. He moved to Albany, New York, in the mid-eighties, where he met my mother, Allison Mortimer, formerly Allison Beckers. Allison grew up in Buffalo, New York and was attending SUNY Albany when my soon-to-be parents met at a local dive bar called Rascals. I am afraid that is about all I know or care to know about those two. They died in a car crash when I was a child, leaving me with my grandmother Thelma, which I know even less about. None of this pertains to my current situation, but I hope it paints my confidence in being independent. I take pride in it.

The squirrel incident happened a few years before the great wreck. It was a defining moment, linking the four of us together. As the only survivor, and eyewitness to the squirrel's demise, I often daydreamed about the similarities of their exit strategies. Did Kieth lie on the asphalt, staring at the sun with beady black eyes, as his wife lay somewhere nearby? Or was it the other way around? Maybe Allison dragged her mangled limbs across the pavement. An undead pantomime, moaning, *Kiiieeeth, Kiiieeeth*. Her innards protruding from her backside, leaving a dark red smear from where she originally landed on the road. Like snail mucus. I would still like to think I had enough in me to grab a rock for them, too. Nobody deserves to suffer like that. Lying twisted and baking in the scorching sun.

I moved to Oswego at some point. Don't ask me to pin the timeline. We will just say it was in my early thirties. It was too close to Allison's birthplace, but I wasn't planning on visiting, so it didn't matter much. I have been here ever since. I left once, when Thelma died back in 2018. We should recognize and give praise for the amazing work of the mortuary cosmetologists. When I approached the casket, I wasn't sure what to expect.

I skipped Kieth's and Allison's funeral under the guise of it "being too soon" as my appointed psychiatrist put it. She knew I just didn't care about going. I still miss Janet sometimes. Thelma looked so happy, lying there and resting after a long existence, some of which included taking care of her dead son's kid. I closed my eyes and listened to see if I could hear her bitching at Kieth from that place people hang out in when they were no longer on this earth. I said my goodbyes and returned to Oswego, a new man. The past is the past. Everyone that had made an indefinite stamp on my timeline was now gone.

* * * *

Now I am standing in my bathroom, staring at my face, trying to see where reality broke and truth reared its ugly head. I leaned in and pulled my left eyelid down with my first two fingers, studying the crease where the eyeball met the flesh. Liquid pooled in the cavity, and I pulled my fingers away and blinked, letting my lid swallow the orb's edge, as the hot salt stung my cheek. How long had I been dead? Was it before or after I dumped the stranger down the garbage shoot? How do you pull such a wild memory from your mind? I thought about the rodent on the road; its twitching tail randomly pointing like a furry-fingered compass. Allison and Kieth. Thelma. The void where the people go when they are not on this earth any longer. I am quite positive my bathroom is not a portal between here and the void. So, I must, therefore, somehow, be partially…here. In the now. Whatever that means. I ran my hand over random objects around the sink, making sure my mind was sane. Rubbing the smaller objects between my thumb and forefinger so I could connect my whirling mind with the current reality. I wasn't sure of the time, so I craned my eyes to scan the couch where the stranger once sat as I walked through the living room to the kitchen. I must admit, I had a moment of guilt that washed over me as I stood in the solitude of my kitchen. *What if the stranger wasn't really dead, either?* He looked and reacted, by a socially accepted standard, as a corpse. Who would allow their head to slam down onto a coffee table like that? To be tied up and tossed down a garbage shoot without a peep. I am only going to tell you what I did next to assure you I am not completely heartless or a lunatic. I could skip it. It doesn't really add any flavor to the outcome of my future, but I would still like to think you would consider keeping a higher opinion of me in the end.

\* \* \* \*

My breath was so loud in the vacant hallway. I wasn't breathing heavily, and I checked my pulse to see if my heart was racing. That was when I noticed it wasn't. Let me clarify. My heart wasn't beating or racing. Its silence became deafening, and I could feel sweat forming between my shoulder blades as I clenched my lungs shut and made my way to the basement steps. My eyes ached as I pressed them against the side of my skull, waiting for a door to swing open. My neighbors seemed like decent people in passing, but it was the middle of the night. They would at the very least check their peepholes to see who the hell was wandering the hallways this late. I clenched my jaw tight as I passed each door, formulating what I would say in the event someone entered the hall. Mary Foreman occupied the last apartment before the stairwell. Although she couldn't have been over forty years old, she looked like Margaret Thatcher towards the end. Mary was the self-appointed building snoop, and the last person I wanted to approach me about my preoccupation. If she had a bug up her ass, I would receive a letter under my door from the landlord about the policy pertaining to disturbances. A written warning, which I would properly ignore, would follow in a separate document. My terms of lease outweigh hers by several years, so the threat, I was sure, would be an "informal formal" way of shutting her up. I stepped past her door and kept my eyes focused on the old push bar metal door that led to the lower confines of the building. I honestly believed at the time that if I didn't look, Mary wouldn't appear. As I gripped the bar and slowly pushed down, I saw myself as Merlin for a moment as the hall remained empty and the door opened with nothing more than a small creak. I closed the door behind me and stared down the dark steps to where the stranger lay swaddled in my clean white designer sheets. The cold cement floor stabbed shards up my calves and I realized I had left my apartment in my socks. I shook my head and scanned the dark room, looking for the garbage shoot. By the way, the burden of proof number two continued as I had yet taken a single breath since I had checked my pulse. What living person can do that?

The basement smelled like damp laundry. Several shelves and racks, covered in dust and cobwebs, lined the dark, moldy walls. Some of the paint, which looked red in the darkness, had peeled away from the cement, exposing the grey brick of the foundation. Several boxes and wooden crates lay scattered about, filled with junk or rolled up newspaper. A stained dirty sheet covered a vehicle in the far-left corner, its shiny metal rims screamed from under its mask, causing an astigmatism. I turned toward the right and found the furnace, as well as the garbage shoot, and a large bin, piled with a cow pattern. A few bags down, the slender form of the stranger jutted out. A long stark white cow dot. I let my eyes adjust for a few minutes before I made my way toward the heap. My body simulated anxiety as the sensation of pounding formed in my chest. I assure you; I checked. There was still no heartbeat. I took slow, arduous steps until I reached him. My knees were screaming from the crouched position of my gate, and I righted my posture as I approached the bin. As I leaned in to listen, I wasn't sure if the end I was inspecting was his feet or head. In the darkness, the bulges looked similar. I took the time to assess, using my hands to poke and prod the packaged stranger. Finding that it was his head that I was fondling, I found his neckline and placed my first two fingers against what I believed was his carotid artery. I know what you're thinking. I don't have a pulse either, so how would I know this guy was dead? Locating a stack of old crates, I broke off a slat of wood and held it in my hand. I pulled a Van Helsing on this guy, but it was the only thing I could think of to prove that he wasn't faking. When I plunged the shard in, I watched for a dark circle forming around the wound. You could imagine my surprise when the sheet remained pure white, even after I yanked the spike. I will save you the gory details of how I returned to my apartment to grab my five-inch serrated bread knife and prove the stranger was indeed deceased. I will, however, tell you I didn't return to my apartment until 4:00 a.m., collapsing on my bed without changing my clothes.

\* \* \* \*

The sun sliced across my bed and arched over my face, burning the thin flesh of my eyelids. During the night, I stopped holding my breath. My chest rose and fell in a steady rhythm. My left leg pulled my midsection to the edge of the bed, and the rest of my body followed suit. As I hobbled out toward the kitchen, I rubbed my face and adjusted my crotch. For a moment, everything felt back to normal. I use the word loosely as I have a hard time assimilating what the term *normal* really defines. When I strolled past the living room, my head arched toward the couch. A wave of relief washed over me as I passed the empty room and stepped into the kitchen. That sensation was short-lived. On the linoleum floor was another body.

## Chapter 3:
## March 26th, 2024, 8:20 am

The recurrence was like a fever dream. A corpse staring at another corpse. I could feel moisture building in the creases of my body. Behind my knees. At the nape of my neck and in the folds of my armpits. I wipe my hands across my cubital fossa, usually referred to as the elbow pits. I learned that technical term in high school biology and refused to use pits to describe any part of the body besides the underarm area. My head throbbed as I stared down at the corpse lounging in my kitchen.

Like the first stranger, the identity was unmistakably male, sans beard. The bodily features in which I had passed over on the first go round with a dead occupant pulled my attention this time. He was much younger than the previous, and his face looked childish in the soft LED lighting. Maybe in his mid-twenties was my guess. His t-shirt, worn and faded, stared back at me from the empty eyes of a skull. Big metal disk plates protruded from the sides of his skull where his ears should be. Chains attached to each disk dangled in front of his well-tailored suit and tie. The apocalyptic background of a destroyed city smoked under a gold-embossed title, Megadeth. His faded jeans were clean and, unlike his shirt, seemed to be brand new. He left both of his Chuck Taylor classic black high-tops untied. The white laces faded into my white linoleum. My eyes returned to his, and I stared into his bright blue eyes, staring into the shadows of my kitchen ceiling.

*How the fuck did you get here?*

I retraced the prior evening in my mind as I stared at the dead kid. Disposed of the body, came home, went back, stabbed the body, came home, passed out. That means the stranger got into my apartment and succumbed to whatever ailment he had while I slept. Impossible. This falls into my Shuffler theory again. This is an unlucky hand here and I can't help but think that someone was trying to tell me something.

I kicked his right foot and watched as it jerked the lower part of his body. He continues to stare at the ceiling, and I trace his stare to see what's so important up there.

"Buddy," I smile down at him, "those shadows ain't where it's at."

This is my technique when faced with surreal situations that I am not mentally prepared to handle. Make jokes. Two dead people in my house in two days. That's a hell of a situation. Walking in circles around the body, I search for a root cause. Blood, a weapon, something. There is nothing. At least nothing that I can see. Thoughts of dragging him down the hallway to the shoot make my shoulders feel heavy. There is also no way, with my luck, that I could escape the nosey warden twice. I would need to get crafty. Let's define crafty.

*Crafty: adjective: Clever at achieving one's aims by indirect or deceitful methods.* Also, *the making of decorative objects and other things by hand.*

Thank you, Webster, for making me feel like a maniac. Sometimes, I feel the shoe fits a bit too snug and I should really look into buying a new pair.

Both definitions fit this situation. One, I am going to need to be clever and deceptive. Two, I am going to be using my hands, although "decorative" would not be the term I would use to describe what I am going to need to turn this corpse into. With a sigh, I step over the body and head towards the coffee maker. The ritual stops for no man, dead or alive.

\* \* \* \*

Being dead is weird, and I have had very little time to dwell on that situation. It's not every day you wake up to find a dead body in your apartment, let alone twice. I have noticed a few things outside of being able to hold my breath indefinitely. For one, I seem to have lost my appetite. Along with that, my sense of taste and smell as well. I listened to the coffee maker percolate and waited for the familiar smell of cinnamon and vanilla. It never came. There is this little coffee shop on the corner and Ninth and Cranberry, Little Dutch Bistro, it's called. They have this flavored coffee called *Cinnamon Spice and Vanilla is Nice.* Small sample bags were being handed out one day, and I obliged. I have purchased a one-pound bag once a month for the last two years. Religiously. Every Monday. First of the month. If you asked me to describe the aroma, I couldn't. It's just heavenly. A magical mix of chocolate, cinnamon, and vanilla bean, concocted by some mystic shaman. He or she probably lives in the basement of that bistro, peeling the sticks of vanilla with a bone fragment. Handcrafting the powders of cinnamon and chocolate in the empty skull of some long-forgotten sacrifice. Yeah, the shit is that good.

I can't decide which is worse; that I may never taste that nectar again, or the failure of my olfactory sense. Yeah, I lost my sense of smell to boot. And there's a dead kid in my kitchen. The last two days can kiss my ass.

\* \* \* \*

I am standing naked in my kitchen holding my five-inch bread knife, tightening and loosening my grip as I stare down at the kid. I left my apartment after finishing my cup of coffee. Do dead people need caffeine? I swear, if I lose one more sacred thing, I am going to go on a rampage. When I approached the counter of Hermen's Hardware with a ten-foot roll of plastic, the cashier asked if I had a discount card before scanning the tag. That was the extent of our interaction. I found it weird that he didn't think it at all odd that I was buying a ten-foot roll of plastic in March. I am trying to stay on topic for the sake of clarity, but I want to note that the clerk had no problem talking to a dead guy. This leads me to believe that he doesn't know I am dead, which could be a possibility. I don't really look the part. I have seen enough zombie flicks to know. Or he is pretending he doesn't know.

We will go down that road momentarily. For now, let me explain how I got rid of the stranger on my kitchen floor. I returned to the apartment and laid the plastic out before undressing the corpse and rolling it to the middle of the plastic. Here we are. Two naked dead dudes ready to have a physical exchange.

\* \* \* \*

I started with the shoulders. I figured starting at a joint would be the easiest route. Wrong. Picking up a saw at the hardware store would have been a smart decision, but here we are, five-inch serrated bread knife in hand. I had to put in some effort for the first arm, and I would be lying if I didn't tell you how surprised I was with the amount of blood contained within a human body. There was a point when I had to stop cutting and pull the edges of the plastic up. I used a half-used roll of duct tape I found in my junk drawer to keep them off the floor, so the blood didn't leak onto the white linoleum flooring. There was another first-time blunder. I forgot to buy garbage bags at the hardware store, and to be fair, if I had added the saw and garbage bags to the purchase, the cashier may or may not have informed the authorities. Lucky for me, I had an enormous collection of avocado-tinted plastic grocery store bags I used for my bathroom trash bin. I removed his legs, starting with the ankles. Then at the knees and then the hips. I never once got sick. I attribute that to the absence of my senses, and that I am dead. Dead people know about other dead people, right? I am not sure exactly what I mean by that.

Packing the bags, I piled them on a bedspread I snatched from my hallway closet. It was a floral-printed hand-me-down from Thelma. It served a greater purpose now. The last bag I stacked onto the pile contained the head. His eyes stared at me through the plastic bag, his mouth gaped open like he was trying to suck in the air. "Little Green Bag" by George Baker Selection began playing in my head. I am aware it is a song about weed, but the green tint of the plastic bags brings forward its catchy bass riff intro. As I gathered up the edges of the taped plastic, circling the tape around the end of the makeshift sack, the clank of drums buried the horror of the room. The snappy beat created a relaxed and almost fun atmosphere. I carefully dragged the blood-filled sack down the hallway, watching each door and listening for the occupants that lingered behind their thin slats. Once again, Lady Luck had shown her teeth. The time dragged as I held my breath. I got the bag down the shoot without spilling a drop. To my shock, the incident hadn't gone awry. I returned to the apartment and took a few bags at a time down to the shoot, spreading the time between trips. The last trip was the flowered sheet. When I finally sat down on the couch and turned on the television, I was exhausted. The morning had turned into midafternoon. I wondered what color Kathleen had decided, hoping it wasn't yet another horrid choice. She was the last thing I wanted to lose faith in. I heard a faint buzz. I stared at the television. My eyes felt heavy and clouded. The buzz again. I traced the sound to my pocket. When I realized it was my cell phone, another sign of my deceased nature reared its head. I couldn't feel the vibration against my leg. As I slid the phone from my pocket, I listened for my breath. Once again, I wasn't breathing. The front display had one notification. It was my friend Kyle.

*Coffee? 5pm?*

I looked at the clock in the upper right corner. 4:12.

*See ya then*, I typed, throwing my phone into the crease of the couch and opening my mouth wide, inhaling to kick my breathing back on.

## Chapter 4
## March 26th, 2024, 5:00 p.m.

The Little Dutch Bistro was unusually busy for a Tuesday. I let the door slam behind me as I scanned the room for Kyle. He was sitting at the far end of the room, by the emergency exit, nursing an oversized white mug. Fat letters in bright gold read "Now this is a mean mug." Two piercing eyes and a crooked smile under the slogan offset the design. The room, a mix of ages, buzzed with conversations, clanking, and slurps. It was an ASMR nightmare. I became overwhelmed immediately and had to close my eyes to center my nerves. There was something else that occurred to me, but we will get into that in a moment. It became apparent during my conversation with Kyle. We will get there.

I approached the counter, keeping my eye on Kyle. When he finally looked up and spotted me, I waved and smiled. He bowed his head and went back to sipping his coffee. I ordered a mug of *Cinnamon Spice and Vanilla is Nice,* sans cream. The Barista, with a shiny plastic name tag reading Jessica, slid the mug and took my money with a smile.

"Your favorite," she winked.

We do not know each other, but I returned the smile to be courteous and walked away, weaving between tables toward Kyle. We have already discussed my loss of senses and, therefore, you probably wonder why I had bothered to waste the money. Well, that's a good question. The easiest answer is to say it was habitual behavior. The complex and true reason was that I was trying to seem like everyone else. Alive. I slumped in the seat, spilling a small amount on my hoodie, and cursed. I think I was more upset that I couldn't smell the cinnamon and vanilla than I was that my black hoodie now had an invisible stain. Kyle cupped his hands around his mug and chuckled at my expense.

"What's shakin'?" Kyle raises the mug and slurps. I immediately become agitated at the amount of jealousy that now flows through me. It's not his fault, though, so I bottled it quickly.

"Ahh. Not much." I lean back. "Just finding dead people in my apartment, chopping them up and throwing down the garbage shoot. You?" That is what I want to say.

"Ahhh, not much." That is what I actually say.

"Well," he slurps again. "You need to get out more, bro."

"I get out plenty." I answered, running my finger over the lip of my mug. Dragging it to my lips, I consume some of my beverage before he catches on and questions why I haven't. He knows *Cinnamon Spice and Vanilla is Nice,* is my favorite, and I am sure he can smell it. I swallow. The lack of odor and flavor is now accompanied by my inability to feel the expected heat. I close my eyes and pretend to be satiated for his benefit. Well, let's be real. It's for my benefit as well. What would he do if he realized I was dead?

Then it hits me. What I mentioned earlier while in line. Is anyone else dead?

* * * *

We have been friends for the better part of three years. I had met Kyle at The Little Dutch Bistro on my first visit. I had known about the cafe for several years but chose the commercialized, over-priced mess. The drive-thru allowed me to get what I needed without the hassle of being around people for long periods of time. There was a large chalkboard on the sidewalk, decorated by some novice, yet talented artist. The drawing, created by what I assumed was washable pastel marker pens, was a large cup, reminiscent of the one Kyle slurps from. The artist placed the cup at the bottom of the chalkboard. Thin line swirls of steam rise from the rim and form into the sale price of the now infamous *Cinnamon Spice and Vanilla is Nice*. I parked my car and walked in, expecting to taste the product and get the fuck out. Kyle was the customer before me and, when I ordered my drink, he looked at me and tried to suppress his laughter. When I asked him what the issue was, he shook his head and walked away. I followed. The details of our exchange that day are unimportant. We didn't really do anything special. We became fast friends over topics of things we do and do not like and the standard personal information. Kyle lives across town in the Hollow Hills trailer park with his mother and little sister. I have never met either of them, but I know their names. Margaret, the mother, and Chelsea, the sister.

I never asked about his father and assumed he wasn't in the picture. Kyle doesn't talk about them much. I have a narrative that I have painted about them. A fantasy, I guess.

Kyle was twelve years old when his father killed his mother and sister. He woke one morning to a loud pop, and when he peeked out of his bedroom door, his father lay sprawled out on the living room floor. A cat chased a mouse across the television. The scene ends with the rodent spinning around and pulling a pan from somewhere within his small body. The cat's eyes widened in horror as the mouse brought the pan down, striking him on the top of his head. A lump in the shape of a mountain formed as the feline wiggled to the ground with a comical look on its face. His father's head, split with something more forceful than cookware, lay open on the rug. His eyes focused across the room in a vacant stare. In his right hand, he held a gun. Shiny, black, and innocent. Kyle had most likely seen the same weapon used on cop shows and spy movies, probably. He traces his father's stare to the couch where he found his sister and mother. Chelsea had little pink bears dancing across her stained white pajamas. His mother had repeatedly threatened to throw them away, complaining that she couldn't use bleach on them anymore. Chelsea would throw a fit and his mother would give up, throwing her hands in the air.

"Fine, look like a bum." She would shout and storm off to find something else to be mad about.

Chelsea had other pajamas, but those were her favorite. So much so that the knees were wearing through. Kyle could see the pink of her right kneecaps peeking through the fabric and would keep his focus there for a moment. He was hoping not to see what had happened. When Kyles' eyes drifted up, his heart pounded against his chest, staunching the air from his lungs. Black circles faded in from his peripherals, and Kyle felt like he was going to pass out. Chelsea's face had somehow disappeared. There was a space there. Matted with hair and clumps of something wet. Various shades of red mixed with white fragments that cut sharply against her chest. Her shoulders slumped forward. Her arms were slack at her sides. The doll she carried lay on the couch next to her. Its dress and plastic peach flesh, painted with Chelsea's blood, stared at the ceiling as if in disbelief.

Kyle's mother leaned crooked against the armrest. Her eyes were closed as if she were napping, but the angle of her body was too exaggerated for comfort. She clenched her stomach, trying to hold her insides from leaking out. Bright red tubes leaked between her fingers and spilled out onto her lap. Kyle ran back to his room and slammed the door, pressing his back against the frail wood that separated his mind from.... *him.*

At least, that's how I imagined it all. His family. The reason why he doesn't tell me anything about them. Nothing personal. Kyle knows the brunt of my story. The silent acceptance of loneliness bonds us, I think.

He is all I have in this shithole town, and I assume he feels the same about me. Whether or not he shares the secret of his murderous father.

I know you were probably hoping for something more, but there isn't. Just my narrative and his. What is worth mentioning is that it resulted in weekly meetups. I now sit with a person who I consider a close and trusted friend. Someone that, eventually, I am going to have to talk to about my predicament. Someone I hope can help me.

* * * *

"So," Kyle sets his cup on the table and folds his fingers together across his chest. "I met up with that girl from the gas station last week." He smiles demonically, showing both sets of teeth, and pulls his bangs away from his eyes.

"How did that happen?" I sit up straight in my chair and scan the room quickly, trying to spot the other undead.

The girl in question is Kimberly Strathert. She was young for my taste. Both of us are much too old for a twenty-three-year-old, in my book, but Kyle had been digging on her for a few months now. I told him my opinion, and he respectfully told me to shut up. She was the manager at Shell, and I don't think I have ever seen her out of uniform. She lived and breathed the petrol of that building.

The backstory. Her dad owned a chain of gas stations up north and when he purchased the old tire shop, he appointed her the head honcho. She had flirted with Kyle one day while I was buying an energy drink, and that set this entire game in motion. He was determined to get with her. By, *get with her*, I absolutely mean his intentions were anything but moral. He was persistent, I would give him that, but she shot him down every time. Maybe he likes rejection. Obviously, his determination didn't go unnoticed.

I abandoned my cup and tapped the table with my index finger.

"I don't need the nasty details, man, but you can kiss and tell the basics."

Kyle's smile somehow spreads wider, almost splitting his face horizontally in two. "Let's just say I had to purchase condoms before we left."

Sometimes, he is so crude. I held up my hand to signal that I indeed had enough of the details. If I had let him continue, how much of his story would be including embellishments on my behalf? Probably a few.

"We have a date next Friday!" He says a little louder than necessary and scans the room to see who cares. No one.

My mind is going elsewhere, but I respond in favor of the venture, knowing it most likely will be short-lived. They are more oil and water than anything.

"That's great, bro!" I lean in and offer my knuckles, which Kyle reaches over and taps against his. He curls his forefinger and thumb around his mug's handle and eyes me from behind the rim as he takes a huge mouthful. I follow suit and sip from my worthless beverage and feel a pang of anger. How could the Shuffler do this to me? Taking away my *Cinnamon Spice and Vanilla is Nice* is taking this whole thing a bit too far. I get the urge to try my luck with Kyle.

"What do you think about zombies?" I blurt out from behind my rim. I try not to stare at Kyle as he pauses and contorts his face in an odd gesture. His top lip curls up on the left side and he closes his right eye.

"What?" he hovers the mug under his nose.

"What do you fucking think about zombies?" I repeat. This time I study his face. Kyle flattens his expression and stares at me with a disappointed frown.

"Lame bro, that's what I think." He shakes his head and slurps his mug.

"Why?" I try to remain calm.

"Dude, they've overdone the story line," he retorts.

"What if you met one in real life?", I continue.

"What if we talk about something cool?" Kyle laughs, and I abandon the conversation. He is the only genuine friend I have, but he isn't ready to hear it yet. He isn't ready to know.

We spent the rest of the evening discussing weed, late night television shows of interest, and, of course, Kimberly. I scan the room every few minutes, trying to spot another dead person. Everyone looks alive, at least at face value. Honestly, I look alive, or people would run, screaming, as they toppled over each other. It's in the movies. It happens like that every time. I also believe Kyle would at the very least stab me repeatedly with the handle end of his coffee spoon before he fled for his life. We are close friends, but no one is close enough to hang around as their bestie eats brains. *Will I do that?* Again, these details also come from movies, and I need to question some of the undead cannon engrained through years of comics and films. *The power of media.* Kyle seems to be unaware of my over the shoulder glances. That or he is pretending. This is the problem with paranoia. If that snowball rolls, watch out. It grows fast and before you know it, you lose control of it. Yes, I know I refer to my situation here as paranoia. I am not saying that I am one hundred percent on board with the label, but I also will not pretend that everything is under my control either. As we see, it clearly is not. As I have said repeatedly, I end up under my bed with a gaping hole in my chest. That's not something I would choose.

Jessica had long left and another barista, whose name I have forgotten, tells us they are closing in five minutes. Don't investigate the Jessica thing. I don't know why I remember her name; I just do. Kyle finishes his coffee, and I discard mine, still half full, into the dish bin, and we part ways, planning to meet again next week. I go home disappointed. The one person who could understand any of this thinks the undead are lame. I sit on my couch watching *The Price is Right* and decide that I will see what happens during this next week. If this all clears up, then whatever. I will consider myself seriously unstable and they should probably lock me up. If I am still undead, then I am going to need Kyle to listen. I am going to need him to be onboard and help me come up with a solution. By the way, he isn't there when I end up under the bed with a hole in my chest. He doesn't find out until he sees it on the news the next day.

I go to the kitchen and turn off the light, plunging the living room into darkness. Standing in the dark, I look at the spot where I had dismembered the stranger. I cross the living room to my bedroom and collapse into my bed, wrapping the sheets around my dead body and hope to God I awaken, sans corpses, and alive.

## Chapter 5
## March 27th, 2024, 9:30 am

The light seeping between the slats of my blinds stabbed at my eyelids. I wish I wouldn't have broken my alarm clock. I need to purchase another one and add it to the mental list of things I have neglected since the two dead strangers interrupted. Rising before the sun is the best way to wake up. It allows a metered adjustment to the approaching hell and its counterparts. I focus on the darkness behind my eyelids. My face buried into one of my overstuffed pillows. The apartment is eerily quiet, and I check my breathing. The slow movement of my chest confirms the reflex, but I can't feel the air enter or exit my nose or mouth. So weird. I know you are waiting for me to get up and check for another stranger. To my shock, and probably yours, I was the sole occupant that morning. Believe me, I checked every nook. I opened every cabinet, and even checked under my bed and the couch, which was too narrow for a body to fit. Confusion gripped me. How do you find a body in your apartment two days in a row? The amount of effort physically and mentally it takes to get your shit together in that situation is overwhelming. I cut one of them into pieces with a bread knife, for Christ's sake! I know, treating the other guy like a vampire isn't exactly lower on the insanity chart. But you can imagine the relief when I found myself alone.

Now, I want to share some information about my revelation, so you focus on why I did what I did next.

I want you to be paying attention. That day, if I had to pinpoint a moment, was the day I fully accepted what was happening to me, I was for sure a walking corpse. With that said, it wasn't the end, as I hoped. There would be more strangers. More, *bread knife moments*, and more *dumping*. It was my lack of good judgment. Choosing to dump them where I did. It was what caused me to end up under my bed that day with a hole in my chest. Again, I am getting ahead of myself, so let me take a moment and explain so we can have a moment of normalcy.

Sure, I couldn't taste the *Cinnamon Spice and Vanilla is Nice,* but I brewed a pot anyway and sat in my living room watching The Weather Channel. I sipped my coffee and tried not to allow my absent senses to ruin the ritual. I also tried not to judge Kathleen's tan pantsuit. With the weather reported to be in the seventies again, I decided I would walk to the mall. It was only two miles, and I thought I could use the time to reflect on what had happened the last two days. While I wandered from store to store, I would watch people to see if my paranoia was getting the best of me. One thing I considered was the possibility that all of this was a psychosis, maybe the onset of schizophrenia. From my understanding of that disorder, the sufferer usually doesn't know they have it. I stuffed the notion into the back of my mind as I dragged myself from my couch, taking a last glance at Kathleen on my way to the bathroom. The pantsuit has pushed me another step closer to giving up on her fashion sensibilities. *See, all this sounds a little normal. Doesn't it?* I understand I may be stretching the term a little and fully accept that "normal" is a vague, open-ended term. But I wasn't using a bread knife to cut up a stranger, so we can agree that there is progress in obtaining the "normal" status label being made.

The shower handle was turned to the far left. The red triangle pushed past its counterpart, signifying the hottest setting. Steam engulfed me as I stood under the scorching water. Although I couldn't feel the pain, I backed away when my skin turned red and reversed the handle the other way. I studied the spots on my upper torso where blisters had immediately formed. There were a few on my chest and two on my left shoulder. I dug my nails into the ugly flesh of my chest, popping the bubbled skin, and letting the water rinse the wound clean. I grabbed my favorite lavender body wash, which I pretend to smell, and washed my body, scrubbing hard against my raw flesh. Stepping out into the foggy bathroom, I walked over to the sink and stared at my distorted reflection in the mirror. My hand wiped across the glass, exposing a dead man staring back. He looked like me, but it wasn't the real me. Not the real Thane. Not anymore. This manifestation of Thane was a hostile takeover. A crazed corpse that chopped up strange dead people in his apartment.

The blisters on my shoulders looked mean, and I pulled the mirrored cabinet open, twisting the doppelgänger's reflection to the side. The tube of Neosporin hid behind old prescription bottles filled with pills I couldn't remember taking anymore. I twisted the cap and squeezed gobs onto my index finger, tilting my head to mark my target. I could have used the mirror, but I didn't want to look at the imposter, so I craned my neck, pressing my eyeballs against the corner of their sockets. After smearing the ointment on my wounds, I tightened the towel around my waist and walked to my bedroom to get ready for my planned excursion. My public mental interrogation. People watching with a sinister motive. Profiling at its finest. I think you get what I mean. Pinpointing the other undead meat puppets couldn't be too hard. I just needed to pay attention.

You don't realize how much you miss something until it gets ripped away. Like the feeling of socks against the bottom of your feet. Or freshly washed jeans pressing down the hair on your legs. That cotton feeling that snuggles your form. The texture of a freshly washed t-shirt or the comforting weight of a zip-up hoodie. The hug of your shoes. These all sound like weird ramblings of a disturbed young man, but I assure you, you're wrong. That old saying "you don't know what you got until it's gone" isn't just a cool Cinderella song. *Oh no, now that jingle is playing in my mind. Give me a minute to reach the chorus so I can shut it down.*

\* \* \* \*

I stepped into the hallway of my apartment building and scanned both sides of the silent corridor. I tilted my head to listen as I took methodical steps toward the stairs. The sound of metal scraping metal split the silence when I pushed the steel bar that locked the door shut. I made a mental note to grab some WD-40 on the way home from the mall. I paused and scanned the hallway, waiting for the warden or another nosey neighbor to peek their head out. When a few minutes had elapsed, I shrugged my shoulders and let the door slam behind me as I skipped down the cement staircase. My shoes echoed off the walls, travelling up the winding staircase toward the roof. I paused at the bottom of the stairwell and inspected the door. Beyond it was the sun, and as of late, that bastard was enemy number one. My eyes have become sensitive over the last few days. There was no way anyone could convince me it wasn't a direct effect of my being a dead dude. Obviously, my eyes could not focus anymore, keeping the proper amount of sun out. Dead. Just like my skin in the shower. Those wounds would not heal. I don't even know why I put ointment on them. Worthless. What was I going to do? Get an infection? *Dead, remember Thane?*

    I pushed the door open, squinting my eyes. I would need to purchase a pair of sunglasses at the sunglass shack. Would I have the same issue with streetlamps and headlights? "Sunglasses at Night," the only hit song I remember from Corey Hart, explodes from my jukebox memory bank. *God, I hate that song.* I will confess, the song is quite catchy. It's his style of singing that I can't handle. He overpronounces his "s" sounds, and I am not sure if it's an impediment or a chosen style, but I hate it. I cupped my right hand over my eyes and looked up at the sky. I headed toward the sidewalk and made my way down Smith and 21st Street. The mall was a few miles away, and I took that time to contemplate my situation. There were quite a few things I considered and thought about during that walk but let me highlight the important points. I think it paints an excellent picture of where I was mentally in that moment during my unfortunate situation.

* * * *

I listened to my sneakers scuff the sidewalk as I watched the lines appear and then disappear under the front of my shoes. Sharp spurts of green would randomly pass through my field of vision, making my eyes trace them before refocusing forward. My mind wandered, only looking up when I reached the corner of each block. Looking quickly from left to right, I would cross the intersection, locking my eyes to the top of my shoes, ebbing forwards and back. If I was truly dead, how could I think?

How could my mind recall songs and things I once enjoyed with such clarity that it made me angry?

How can I feel angry?

How can I feel…anything?

How long had I been dead?

I couldn't recall a specific moment when it went from the living Thane to…*this*. The stranger that inhabited my body and kicked the original Thane out. Is that what has happened? Am I an imposter? Was this some weird type of body snatcher scenario? Was I being overtaken by a natural bacterium that had somehow escaped the population, or at least me? If Kyle couldn't tell I was dead, then how could I expect to see it in others? Maybe this has been going on for decades. Thousands of people slowly turned into walking corpses, unsure of their purpose, unaware of the sickness that eats them from inside out. These thoughts are the stuff of movies. Although I don't believe it to be some crazy space related incident, I can't rule any wild theories out. I would end up calling Kyle later and having an insane conversation where he questioned my sanity. We will get to that later.

What happens when, or if, my brain stops functioning like the real Thane? That's a weird question, is it? Let's approach this from another angle. What if I suddenly get the craving for things I shouldn't? Like brains? Again, movie legends. But it is worth pondering. I always found the truth lies somewhere between fact and fiction. Will I lose my voice too? Start mumbling incoherent garble as I pace my apartment, waiting for some unlucky bastard to stumble in and check on the weird tenant in 3B? The other thing that wormed its way in, no pun intended, was the effects of death itself. Would I eventually decay? Maybe those burn blisters that formed in the shower were the beginning of that phase? Albeit they were the result of scalding stream of water. It doesn't dismiss the notion that the flesh may not heal. This would lead to the spreading of decay. If this became a reality, there would be a point where I would have no option but to stay inside. Stuck to the four walls of my eight hundred square foot apartment. Did I really think this could become my reality? Yes, and for a short time, that life did become a reality. I assume that if I had not wound up under the bed with a gaping hole in my chest, this existence would have continued. For how long, I can't say. It is safe and realistic to say that I would have run out of money. Without being overdramatic, one could easily see how all this would have turned out the same. It just tracks down to *when*, not *how* or *if*.

I took a shortcut, crossing the street at Hadel and Ninth, cutting through Mason Park. The sun illuminated the open field, shining off the aluminum bleachers that surrounded the public baseball field. My direction pivoted as I left the sidewalk and entered the grass. I wanted to shorten my exposure time. There were usually only a few people in the park, but right now, there were too many. I picked up the pace as a woman rounded the walkway that circled the ball field. To my far left, an elderly man sat on a park bench. His upper body leaned toward the right, and I slowed my steps so I could assess whether he was alive. His arm jerked, and he sat upright with a startled look on his face, scanning the park. Our eyes connected and he averted his face, looking across the open yard. I stuffed my hands into my hoodie and picked up my pace, hoping to beat the woman around the bend of the dugout. It was hard to keep from looking back. I could sense his eyes on me. Did he know? Could he sense I wasn't breathing? I checked. I wasn't. When I reached the edge of the turn and rounded the back end of the dugout, the old man had disappeared. I stopped and scanned the park. He had vanished. The sound of footsteps and heavy breathing jerked me back to reality.

"Good morning," the woman panted as she jogged past me. She was wearing a windbreaker and tight black joggers that showed off her athletic figure. I bowed my head, trying to hide my face as she passed me and continued around the back of the pitcher's mound. I watched her auburn hair bounce, swaying back and forth across her shoulders as she continued down the path that circled the diamond. She reminded me of a rat in a cage.

Yup, The Smashing Pumpkins, "Bullet with Butterfly Wings" immediately rang through my head. If you know the song, you know. The bald lead singer stares through thin black eyeliner from the recess of my mind. He sways back and forth, wearing a long black trench coat and strumming a melting guitar. To be fair, that was a later look for him. He was still wearing band shirts and had a full head of hair when that song came out.

I can argue that we are all rats in a cage, but this lady is more rodent than most. What she is doing is the epitome of insanity. You know the definition. Doing the same thing, expecting a different result. I got news, Brenda, you're still gonna die.

I scan the field for the old man again, somewhat disappointed when he is nowhere to be found. This made me wonder if it was a hallucination. I stared at the empty bench for a moment before reverting my attention to the woman coming around the bend again, her attention focused on her feet. I paid homage to the old man, disappearing toward the far end of the bleachers.

## Chapter 6
## March 27th, 2024, 1:25 pm

The parking lot came into view as I climbed the hill on the east end of the mall. I had to shield my eyes from the sun's rays reflecting off the vehicle's windshields. My hand slid up under my shirt and pressed against my left breast. I closed my eyes and waited for my heart to pulse against my palm. There was a sense of anxiety, although I could feel nothing. I would love the details to be clearer, but I don't know how else to explain it. Most of what makes me human, including my emotions, is gone. The things that remain, like this slight sense of anxiety, are fading. I pinched my eyelids tight and listened through my hand. Nothing. The realization of what was happening still had not secured itself in my mind. At that point in my predicament, I still held a certain state of denial, masked as hope, or maybe a dream state. I remember standing on the crest of the parking lot, watching people enter and leave the different sections of the building, each stranger living within their own existence, their own truth. Some were having the best day of their lives, while others suffered through whatever ailment afflicted them. Each individual glues on a mask. In truth, everyone is dead under there. Rotting away. Every muscle pulling the corners of their mouth into manic smiles that others accept as happy. It's all bullshit. Somewhere within that moment was the birth of a trigger. The need to know. I wanted to find others like me. The ones walking around already, or nearly dying. How would I approach them? Get nose to nose, fists balled and ready for conflict. Calling them out on their bullshit facade. *Our* bullshit facade.

First off, that hypocrisy would be insulting. Calling them a liar as I walk around faking normality for myself? Furthermore, what would their reaction be? Would they shake their heads, pointing their fingers into guns?

"You got me, chief," pinching one eye shut like a highway robber and smiling.

My imagination blossomed into chaos as images of fingers digging into the fake flesh masks, tearing away strips to expose the rotting, insect-filled decay underneath. Screams cascade over the crowds as the cry echoes down the corridor. Everything becomes still as every head turns in our direction. The faces remain placid as they stare wide eyed. Fake smiles spread across their face as the ghoulish monstrosity bellows to the ceiling before charging the first onlooker. The crowd watches, and the creature topples the victim over and tears into the flesh of the face and gnaws on their cheekbone. There are no cries of protest or pain. No one runs. No one reacts. I watch as the monster makes its way through the crowd, devouring random strangers until it disappears around the corner entrance of the food court. A field of blood, organs, and unnaturally twisted mounds marks its path to the far end of the building. I apply the adjectives to myself and wonder how long it will be before I am chewing on Kyle's head?

I step onto the blacktop and walk toward the main entrance. As people pass by me, I overhear fragments of conversations. Upcoming plans for dinner. How unbelievable it was that her husband cheated on her. How sales really weren't sales, just a corporate exercise in income espionage. I watched the top of my shoes as I took them all in. There were a few times I wanted to look up. Stare into their eyes and wait for them to admit it. Come clean so I can, at the very least, feel like I am not entirely alone. But I don't. I just continue to listen to the random passersby as I make my way to the entrance. It was easier to gawk at strangers in a large crowd. I pulled the corners of my mouth up, pulled the door open, and walked into the food court.

\* \* \* \*

Have you ever tried to eat beef Lo Mein when you can't smell, taste, or feel anything? Let me say that the reality of the act is harder to discern than you would think. Part of you wants to describe it. A mouth full of worms, perhaps. A mix of slimy strings and thick chunks. In reality, it's nothing. No sense of feeling, remember? So, no feeling of slime or something resembling worms. No sense of thick chunks split and gnawed between my molars. The familiar combination of odors associated with Chinese fast food. Soy sauce, spices, and oils. The burning taste of salt. All gone. I push mouthful after mouthful of nothing into my maw and let it slide down my dead throat, unaware of whether I am choking on the useless protein. Staring into the passing sea of strangers, I squeezed my fingers around my throat. Nothing seemed to be lodged, and I was still not breathing. My eyes feel dry in their sockets. It is from my intense gawking; I am sure, but I am not entirely sure because I am dead, and dead things don't create tears. I scan the crowd for the telltale signs of my community. The engraved details from movies and literature concerning the dead. A forward gait in their walk. The absence of the rise and fall of their chest plate. Blank stares with unblinking eyes. Most of all, there is a strange notion. I know I have said there are no senses, and I am not saying this is acceptance, but it is a notion. A connection. I felt it when I wrapped up the man on my couch. I felt it when I cut up the stranger in the kitchen. His eyes stared back at me from the little green bag, forgiving me for doing what I had to do. I don't know what to call it. It is surely a connection that is only between dead things. I think. My connection with Kyle is different. Moreso now that I am what I am. Our friendship is based on a kinship. Truths. Save that I now harbor a gross secret.

\* \* \* \*

I walked through the hallways of the mall for several hours, peeking into store fronts and feigning interest through heavily advertised windows. The various strangers adorned with designer clothes and sticky perfumes sipped from white-capped paper cups, oblivious to my inspections. Fucking liars is what they are. Or just idiots. That could be the very distraction. The lulling of one into a false sense of knowing. It's either the other dead pretend to not notice I am dead, trying to hide from me what they themselves are, knowing damn well they know I know, or they have blended in, and I am not yet able to detect them. They go on living a pretend life as if the great Shuffler had never drawn their immortality card. On a side note, there was a dark moment that would plague the better part of the next few days. I stood at the entrance of Leaps and Bounds Toy Store. To be fair, it was next to Victoria's Secret Pink Outlet. In my younger years, I would sit on the bench in the middle of the walkway and study the women and men that would frequent Pink. I felt like a perv watching strangers shopping for intimates. The husbands, with flushed cheeks, try their hardest not to look at the low-cut lingerie. Keeping their eyes on the floor when passing female shoppers. Nodding at the other husbands. A brotherhood of an uncomfortable necessary duty.

    Shoppers made their way around my corpse. Tugging along smaller versions of themselves. The giant toy displays, strategically placed to funnel the crowd, rose to the archway of the entrance. This is when something sinister reared its nasty head. Some of these people are dead like me and in their grasp was the wrist of a child. Take that in. A child. The horror of this revelation consumed me. To be honest, if a chill could have climbed my spine, it would have. I watched as adults shuffled around like angry bees, snatching up toys and bending to show them to their children. Their little faces lit up, showing the proof of life, as they hugged the sharp-edged boxes and stuffed animals. A few of the older children had hardened looks, wanting to be anywhere else, like at their friend's house or on their computers, creating scenarios of war. The parents ignored the teenagers' unenthused faces and rushed around, pretending not to be bothered by the price, which was over sixty percent of its value. Some adults drew me in more than I would have liked. A connection. A dead one. The others seemed to be oblivious to their placid reaction to the chaos. The flat expression as they, with a hand gripped tight around a child's, watched the frenzy. Watching what the others were doing, they would bend down with a random toy and smile as their child jumped up and down, smiles splitting their faces. There was nothing more that I could have wished for at that moment than a sense of anxiety. A full-blown panic attack. I wanted to scream and run from the mall, blasting through the doors into oncoming traffic. End this insanity. But I am dead. Chances are that the car would throw my body fifteen feet, and I would lie there no worse for wear. Maybe they would run over me. Mangling my body under the fender. Ripping chunks of flesh from my decaying chest. I would sit up, like in the movies, the living screaming in terror as the mall erupted into chaos. But I just stood there and watched. There was a state of confusion that needled its way to the forefront. I am convinced that I am dead. With one hundred percent certainty. Unfortunately, I cannot be as certain about anyone else. I needed clarity. A sense of foundation. I needed my friend. First, I needed to get the fuck out of the mall.

* * * *

There was a tiny sense of shame, leaving those children with their dead parents. But I didn't hold the cards. People can blame the Shuffler. After all, he is the great and powerful Oz, right? As I approached the crest of the hill, I looked back toward the entrance. The sun was dropping to the horizon of the roof, splitting a single ray that stabbed toward the clouds. It would be dark soon, and I needed to get home. I pulled out my cell phone and opened my message app. I found my previous text to Kyle and pecked at the keys.

*Can I call you in a couple of hours?*

Only a few seconds elapsed before three dots danced across a bubble.

*Yeah, when are you thinking? Make it quick cause I am meeting Kimberly at 7:30.* Three smiling devil emojis follow the response.

I check the clock and frown. It read 6:25. I didn't want to talk with him until I was in the solitude and safety of my apartment.

*Hit me up when you're done.* I tap the screen a little harder than I want to.

*It will be late, but sure thang!* He responds.

I shove the phone into my pocket and head down the back side of the hill. I remember that I still need to stop at the hardware store for that WD-40. Maybe I'll grab a saw while I am at it.

## Chapter 7
## March 27th, 2024, 8:45 pm.

    I stepped into the blacked-out kitchen and placed the plastic bag on the counter, along with the receipt for the can of lubricant and a pack of Blackjack gum. I would mark the WD-40 on the receipt and send it to the main office for reimbursement. Screw them, I am not paying for their negligence. That's fifteen dollars I couldn't part with, not with what was coming. While my eyes took time to adjust to the darkness, my mind ran scenarios of what was next to come. One of my major concerns was Kyle's response to finding out his best friend was a corpse. Although I want to believe he would shrug his shoulders and give me that curt smile, staring at me through his stringy black bangs, the truth is I don't know how he is going to react. As well as I would like to think I know Kyle, there is a lot of grey between us. As I have said, I consider him to be my best friend. We have shared things, human things. As many as two people can, on a set schedule once a week. The grey area is a vast desert of topics and truths that we have secretly agreed to avoid. Details about each other that would serve no purpose to share. Things that may drive us apart if they escape the desert. The truth about my parents' demise. The joy I get when I picture Allison crawling across the pavement. Skin sliding behind her mangled legs, leaving a bright red trail, the red ochre of her soul against the painted yellow lines that trace the middle of the road. The empty void behind Kieth's eyes watching his wife fight her way to an already lost cause, tache noire staring back. Kyle knows I am dark and that I have an unusual distaste for my family, but these details may cross a line that even Kyle can't look past. He keeps his secrets as tightly wrapped as I keep mine. His mother and sister. His father. My narrative about them. I find it funny that the two topics I chose are family related. The telltale of a bitter soul. Except, last time I checked, corpses don't have souls.

Coffee cups and plates stacked in the sink remind me of how much I have neglected household chores. I want to feel guilty about my off-colored inner dialogue about the upkeep of the apartment building, but I don't. As I make my way to the living room, there is a sudden change in the air. A heaviness. The atmosphere felt like a rain cloud. The remaining sense of anxiety flooded forward. It started as a small tingle, then cascaded into a hum that vibrated up my spine and then rested on my forehead. I was not alone in the apartment. I pretended to hold my breath as I waited for my heart to pound against my chest. After ten minutes, I gave up and paced my living room. If there was someone here to do harm, they would have made themselves known. The same analogy applies if they were here to rob me. I am three floors up in a small apartment with nowhere to hide. Confrontation would be inevitable. That leaves one alternative. Another dead body.

The man submerged in my bathtub had to be in his mid-forties. His thin, pale body, suspended under the glass surface of the water, reminded me of Han Solo encased in Carbonite. Wrinkles and an opaque quality marked the flesh on his joints and hands. He wasn't bloated, and though from the many crime shows I have watched, he should have been. It looked like he had been in my tub for the better part of the day. His short salt and pepper hair swayed with the micro movements of the water. His pubic hair and genitalia oscillated and bobbed in slow motion between his legs like a swollen worm. I had to force myself to look away.

*How the fuck did you end up here?*

I bent down on my knees next to the tub, resting my chin on the edge of the cold white porcelain. My imagination filled in the gaps where my senses have failed. The smell of moisture. Heaviness dipped in the fragrance of this expired stranger, now playing dead man float in my bathtub. I reached my hand over the edge and poked his chest. The water rippled as he sank slightly and then tilted a little to the side before becoming still. I stared at his face until my mind had righted itself. I needed to get rid of him. I should have bought the saw, I know. A few things about this one had troubled me. One, he was already naked and submerged in water. A quick glance around proved their absence, which made the situation worse. Where did he get undressed? Two. Who filled the tub and why? The obvious guess would be him. That leaves why? Then the big one. Why the fuck did he choose my apartment?

There was a consideration that wormed its way into my mind. A sinister birth of a pattern. Did they all know each other? Was this some type of weird cult thing? Pick a random stranger and die in his apartment?
*Too commercial. Too HBO.*

But did they know each other? There would be no way of figuring this out now. I had dumped the first guy, then played Van Helsing on him. The second one, I dismembered and dumped on top of the first one. So here we are. It was here that I finally took the plunge. I reached into my front pocket and pulled my cell phone. I tap the screen and thumb through to Kyle's contact. With one hand, fingertips deep in the dead man's water, and the other hovering over my best friend's contact, I ran through the various scenarios of how this would play out. I felt trapped. Damned if I do, damned if I don't. Kyle would either shrug his shoulders and roll up his sleeves, or the cops would be here. I knew him well enough to know that he wouldn't just walk away from this. Three people were dead, and, for all he knew, by my hand. When I pressed on the contact, my eyes were still closed, and I listened as the ringtone echoed. Each beep cascading into a deafening roar. I was about to throw the phone into the water to escape the sirens when I heard a click and Kyle's voice.

"What's up, bro?" He coughed. Sounding like he was half asleep, or high. I opened my eyes and cleared my throat. "I need you to come over to my place, please." His silence made the room buzz, and I immediately regretted asking.

"Really?" he cleared his throat again. "You have never asked before. Everything okay?" There was a sense of concern in his voice, but I could tell he was trying to keep his response neutral.

"There's a dead body in my tub."

More silence.

There was a hard click before the line went dead and I dropped my phone. The clank reverberated off my skull as I collapsed to the floor and closed my eyes. My world was spiraling down into a void. Somewhere that I could hold myself until the cops arrived. Maybe they would come into the bathroom and the shock of the situation would make them draw their weapons. I would jump up, a crazed zombie hungry for flesh, and they would discharge several rounds into me until I stopped moving. Finally silent. To be clear, this isn't the end where I end up under my bed with a hole in my chest. I know most of you are paying attention enough to know that we are in the bathroom, so we are not in that part of my situation yet.

I was in the fetal position when I heard the pounding on my door. I lay on the floor and balled my fists, pressing them into my chest. The pounding became more frantic, and I assumed they would kick in the door, eventually. The pounding grew louder, smashing off the walls of my skull. I dragged myself to my feet and waddled out toward the kitchen. When I leaned my forehead against the front door, the pounding jostled my head, bouncing it off the wooden frame. I unlocked the door and swung it open, ready for the onslaught of officers to tackle me. Kyle threw his hands in the air and barged past me, heading for the living room. I turned around and slammed the door behind me.

Kyle stuck his thumbs in his front pockets and whipped his head to the side, throwing his bangs and exposing his face. His eyes were stern. The corners of his mouth quivered slightly. Kyle's voice held a concern that informed me he hadn't quite decided yet. What he believed he had heard me confess. He still may be on my side. Kyle leaned in and gave me a hard stare.

"What the fuck is going on, Thane?"

## Chapter 8
## March 27th, 2024, 11:15 pm.

We stand in the bathroom looking down at the floater. Kyle is leaning his weight on one leg, hands stuffed in his front pockets. Confusion and anger radiate from his face.

"What is this?" The low tone in his voice echoes off the porcelain. The weight of the moment suppressed the regular excitement of his personality.

"It's a dead body." I say. The muscles in my eyes strain as I press them against the corners of their sockets. I am trying to keep control over the situation, although I am just as confused and angry as Kyle. This is body number three with no explanation of who they are and why they chose my apartment to end their lives. Now, I have dragged my closest confidant into this mess with nothing of substance to provide. He will have questions, and I will have no answers. Kyle shifts his weight to the other leg and opens his mouth to speak but cuts himself off by twisting his lips shut.

"He was here when I got home." I add.

Kyle drags his hands from his pockets and folds them across his chest, nodding as if he will accept my explanation. He does.

"So," he turns to me and stares at the side of my head. His eyes burn my temples, and I get that small tick of anxiety that climbs up my spine. It is the only thing that makes me think I could be semi-alive. If there is such a state. My sanity says otherwise.

"Are you asking me to assist in the disposal of unwanted material in your bathroom?"

The delivery of his question caused the anxiety to pause at my throat, wrapping its claws and squeezing.

"Why are you talking weird?" my voice squeaked, wiggling its way from underneath the grip of anxiety. Kyle pulls his cell phone from his pocket, pinching it between his thumb and forefinger. He shakes it in my face. My eyes study the phone as his fingertips turn white.

"They hear everything." Kyle spins the phone into his palm and pockets the device.

I nod and pretend to take a breath. The anxiety relaxes and dribbles down my dead esophagus, making its way into my belly. Calling Kyle served two purposes. Fear and desperation consumed a greater part of the equation. There was a smaller part that wanted someone else to take the lead. Guide me out of this predicament. My *situation*. Kyle turns his attention back to the floater.

"So, you have no idea who this dude is?" He bites his bottom lip.

Again, I shook my head, stuffing my hands in my front pockets to give the illusion of helplessness. Kyle doesn't need to know that I have handled this twice before. I take a pretend breath.

"Maybe we can bring him somewhere exclusive." I am surprised at how calm my voice is. Letting my guard down could tip off Kyle, so I cough and then rub the back of my neck, feigning an unease with my solution. If my cheeks could have flushed, they would have. It was one of the few times during my situation that I thanked God I was dead. Kyle tilted his head and dropped the corners of his mouth down.

"If we could get him downstairs without being noticed," He paused and shifted his weight to his other leg again. "I know a place where he could rest easy."

The luck I had disposing of the first two bodies was, to put it mildly, pure chance. I didn't feel confident testing it again. I could picture it, the building warden coming out into the hallway. We are hefting a long bundle that could be mistaken for nothing else but a body. Or, worse still, several bloody bags. She would scream, stumbling back into her apartment. The sounds of sirens would soon follow. I would spend the rest of my long undead life in a cell, alone, with the guilt of ruining my best friend's life. That's what ran through my mind at that moment. I don't think I would have cared as much if I knew then how I would end up. *Stuffed under my bed with the gaping hole in my chest.* There was a type of envy harbored for the submerged stranger in my tub. I cannot explain it, except to say that as a fellow dead man, he had the better position. The serenity of silence. The weightless calm. No obligation to assist in our plight. He was, for all intents and purposes, an innocent bystander. I am being liberal with the term "innocent." After all, it is because of this fucker killing himself in my apartment that we are in this situation to begin with. As I watch him hover in my tub, I run through my inventory of disposable bed sheets. There are none that I am willing to part with. There is, however, an abundance of green tinted plastic grocery bags under my sink, which hold no value. The song "Little Green Bag" once again worms its way up into my decaying brain and I tap its bass line with my foot against the cold tiles of my bathroom floor. Kyle looks down at my foot and scrunches up his face. My solution surprises even me as I open my mouth, looking toward the bathroom window next to the toilet.

"We will toss him out the window." I say matter-of-factly.

Kyle widens his eyes and turns down his mouth, nodding with approval. He wouldn't respond well to the next part. I leave him standing there as I head to my kitchen for the proper tools. I return with a bundle of green bags tucked under my left arm. In my right hand is the five inch serrated bread knife. Kyle flattens his expression, staring at the silver curved teeth.

"You cannot be serious." He responds flatly.

At that moment, I didn't think I could have been any more serious. I shut the bathroom door and drop the plastic bags next to the toilet. I reach my free hand between the ankles of the floater and flip the drain.

\* \* \* \*

Throughout the ordeal, Kyle had lurched enough to empty five human stomachs. I saved him from some of the turmoil and kept working as he regained composure with his arms crossed over the rim of my toilet. Between his moaning and the wet sound of tearing muscles, the last nerve that remained in my body threatened to expire. I had to remind myself that Kyle was here, sacrificing himself by helping me dispose of the stranger. In the end, I am dead. I can sit forever in a cell. It would even be fair to say that it was the best place for me. But Kyle didn't deserve repercussions concerning my situation. There was a full life waiting for him out there.

I vaguely remember "Into the Great Wide Open" by Tom Petty ringing in my mind. Although I am not one hundred percent sure, it's a strong ninety-nine. I say this because I strongly recall sawing off one of the strangers' arms while whistling the chorus. I had packed most of the body parts in the green plastic bags and was in the middle of retrieving more bags when I heard a knock at my door. Kyle looked up, wide eyed, from the toilet. His mouth gaped open like a fish. A string of mucus dripped from his bottom lip as his bulging eyes jerked back and forth between me and the front door. I raised my index finger to my lips and stood frozen in the kitchen. The knock repeated, followed by the voice of my elderly neighbor, Kenny.

"What the hell is going on in there, Thane?" The words gargled between deep breaths. "I am trying to sleep."

The old man was probably leaning on his oxygen tank, pressing his eye near the crack in the door frame.

"Sorry, Kenny," I pumped my index finger in front of my mouth, puckering my lips at Kyle. "Just trying to catch up on cleaning."

The old man stood silent in the hallway while we stared at each other. There was some grumbling and then Kenny knocked on the door.

"Don't be sorry, Thane, just keep it down or I'm gonna call the landlord, Capisce?"

I relaxed my shoulders and closed my fist, biting my first knuckle.

"Yes, sir." My voice echoed through the kitchen. There were a few more grumbles as he made his way down the hall. I waited for Kenny's door slammed shut before I walked to the wall that split our apartments. I pressed my ear to the thin barrier and closed my eyes. When his television crackled to life, I returned to the bathroom and knelt on the cold floor next to the dissected and partially bagged stranger. Kyle wiped his gullet and crawled next to me. I was thankful that my sense of smell had not returned. I could imagine Kyle smelled like he looked. His pale face trembled, moisture speckled his forehead. Sweat matted his hair, flattening it against his oddly shaped dome.

"Want me to finish this before we toss it out the window?" My voice was calm. A technique I had picked up while binging True Crime shows. Kyle shook his head and stood up and headed towards the living room. The rest of the job took another hour. Some of which was spent doubling up the bags so Kyle wouldn't be able to see the strangers' parts. Taking special care with the head was paramount, so I added a third bag. I couldn't risk Kyle losing his shit, setting off Kenny again. I would then have to take matters into my own hands. Chopping up bodies of dead strangers is one thing. It is another thing to be the person causing the death.

Kyle remained on the couch as I opened the window and scanned the grounds three stories down and then tossed the bags into the bushes below. The pile wasn't as large as I thought it would be, and the dim lighting helped hide the already green bags. My bathroom window faced the woods that spanned three acres behind our apartment complex. A small drive ran the back length of the building, and my plan was to toss the bags out the window, then pull the car around to retrieve them. Clean and easy. At the time of conception, the plan sounded solid. I was not expecting Kyle's reaction and, in hindsight, hefting the body down three flights of stairs might have been the better option. But here we are.

Kyle lay sprawled out on my couch with his ankles crossed and his forearm over his eyes.

"You all good?" I tried to sound more concerned about his wellbeing than the body parts piled in the bushes.

"I'm sorry, bro." He grumbled from under the crook of his elbow.

"No harm, no foul." I offered, keeping the anxiety from resurfacing. "But we have to get going. We can't leave those bags out there for long."

Kyle swung his feet to the floor and twisted his lower body upright. He slapped his palms on his knees and stood up, giving me a smile. I pretended not to notice how sickly he looked as I snatched my keys off the counter and headed for the front door.

"Let's finish this," Kyle grunted and followed me into the hallway.

* * * *

Kyle opened the hatchback of his beat-up Ford Taurus wagon. He had cut several black garbage bags and laid them flat, weighing them down with a trowel on one side and a shovel on the other. We piled the bags in the center of the bag, careful not to touch the ceiling or the back of the seats. As we headed toward the highway, we discussed his disposal plans. Kyle regained some color to his face and his hands had stopped shaking. Both were good signs, knowing what was about to transpire. Admittedly, he expresses that this was, for him, the easier part of the job and I didn't argue. There was a small nagging in the primitive part of my brain that he had come to this conclusion because I would do most of the digging. Rightfully so, in all honesty. I have asked my friend to do something without explanation that if it were anyone else, they would have called the authorities. He didn't even hesitate. I can dig the fucking hole.

There was no one on the highway. The landscapes blurred by as I listened to the tires hum against the asphalt. Kyle droned on about the plot of land where we would dispose of the stranger. It was a twelve-acre plot of abandoned farmland owned by his uncle Steven, which he hadn't seen in over eight years. It was an unexpected and unwanted inheritance from a relative that Kyle didn't know. His uncle had tried to sell the property for several years and gave up a few years back when he moved to Montana. Now, his land sits vacant. Unattended. Unmanaged. Unaware that two dudes are going to dig a hole to bury the chopped body of a stranger. One of which is his nephew. Kyle had also said that if someone had come along, he would tell them it was his uncle's property, and if they were to call him, Steven would shake his head and ask what his nephew was up to. The story would be that they were camping on a budget. Kyle's description of the property made it impossible to dispute. As long as they didn't see the enormous hole, or the individually wrapped body parts in the dark green bags. The vehicle bounced down the highway and I checked the dashboard analog clock. It was nearly four a.m. The sun would be up around six a.m. We would have a little over an hour to work after finding a spot. The anxiety tingled from the depths of my belly as I watched the yellow strip in the center of the road.

"Do we have enough time?" I heard my voice bounce off the windshield. Kyle gripped the steering wheel and clicked his tongue between his teeth, tilting his head.

"Yeah, I mean, we will be deep in the property, so the only thing that could see us would be a low-flying plane or something."

I nodded and rested my chin against my fist and turned my attention to the shoulder of the road. The multicolored stones mixed against the black asphalt, lulling me to sleep. I heard a soft click. The soft voice of Stevie Nicks filled the cabin, informing us that "lightning only happens when it's raining," and as I dozed off, I questioned the validity of her assumption. After all, she had never been dead.

## Chapter 9
## March 27th, 2024, Time Unknown.

The stones on the shoulder of the road painted a mosaic in earth tones that blurred beneath the sharp white soles of my Chuck Taylors. The sun assaulted the back of my neck as the strap of my backpack dug into the muscle between my neck and shoulder. Every few minutes I would shift the weight, using my thumb and wrist as leverage. Empty road stretched out for several miles, hazing into a blur of black and green vapor in the distance. It gave the illusion of a dystopian Armageddon. A place ruled by men like Max Rockatansky. A world ending in a mirage. Walking home from school wasn't the ideal situation, but it allowed me to be with myself for a while. When I say that, I mean alone. The kind of alone that digs deep and blurs out the surrounding context of the world around you. The natural stimulus fading from your mind. A place where nothing matters. My shoes allocated the only perception of time and distance. Passing under and moving me forward to my destination, that was set on autopilot. Flashing images of my parents broke my serenity. Characters playing a role. Pretending to love one another. Hugging and holding hands as they walked down the empty road before me. Fading in and out of the vapors, corrupting the world behind them. The smile on their faces melted, creating a blood coated grimace. Overlapping closeups of them vibrant and alive, mixing with landscape images of a mangled car. Gore smeared over yellow stripes. The torso of Allison crawling. Her elbows scrape against the chipped asphalt, leaving bright red dots in their wake. She dragged her entrails down the center of the road towards Kieth's corpse. His empty stare coaxing her forward. The image flashes. A subliminal burn of Thelma silently laughing in her casket. Her teeth gleaming in negative exposure. Another flash. My parents' hands twisting together in a tight grip as they press their free hand firmly on my shoulders. But that boy isn't me. He is a dead stranger on my couch. He is a dead stranger spread out on my kitchen floor. The imposter is a floating, engorged cock writhing between the legs of a suicide in my bathtub. Those three are the enablers of this toxic relationship that ended with blood smeared across hot asphalt. They are the enablers of an influential stigma that saved the squirrel when I couldn't save them.

    I shift the weight of my backpack and watch the stones blur past in my peripheral. So, when did the imposter know I would die? When was it foretold that I would chop up corpses? Dump people down garbage shoots or bury body parts of a stranger in barren fields with the only person I love? There I said it. I loved Kyle. He was the only real person who had ever been there for me. There was a thud that emanated from the right side of my head as I suddenly jerked to the side and then forward.

## Chapter 10
## March 28th, 2024, 4:30 am.

Brush and branches, illuminated by the headlights, clanked against the sides of the windows. I rubbed the side of my head and Kyle tapped my cheek.

"We're here." He smiled.

I found a small knot where my head had bounced off the window when Kyle turned onto the dirt road that led us to the future burial ground. Another piece of personal damage that won't heal.

Have you ever dug a hole large enough to bury ten to twelve bags of body parts? It is a lot harder than you would expect. There is a sense of difficulty that comes along with digging a hole, but until you do it, by hand. You do not know just how grueling it is.

We bounced down the dirt road and I rubbed my face and then checked the clock on the dash. Four-thirty.

"We got to move, man. The sun will be up soon." I closed one eye and rubbed the side of my head again, trying to quell the ache.

Kyle looked like a psycho as he grinned from ear to ear and shook his head.

"We have plenty of time, bro. As I said before." He tilts his head toward me and looks up from under his eyebrows. "No one around for miles." He turns his attention back to the dirt road, his head jostling back and forth like a bobble head toy.

When he stopped the vehicle and shut off the ignition, we sat for a few minutes as his headlights cut into a vast empty field. I studied the perimeter of the headlights and looked at the ground. The tall blades of grass sheltered the hard work ahead. Kyle tapped the steering wheel, then popped open his door and climbed out. He reached down near the door jam and popped the back hatch.

"This hole won't dig itself." He smiled and headed toward the back of the car.

There was a glow on the horizon just above the tree line. The sun was coming and a moan of disappointment echoed across the field. The hole was only five feet round and approximately four feet deep. It was going to have to do. Kyle leaned against a tree near the front of his car, picking his nails. To my surprise, Kyle helped for the first half hour. We were making good progress, and I expected us to be finished and heading home by now. I had the shovel and Kyle took the trowel. Having the weaker tool, Kyle gave up at the first sign of blisters forming on his palm. I didn't check for gashes when Kyle climbed from the hole and headed toward the car, shaking his hands in protest. It didn't matter. I wouldn't feel them. As I climbed from the hole, the first rays of light sliced the tops of the trees and turned on the lights of the world. I clapped my hands together and signaled for Kyle to back the car into position. He climbed into his Taurus, and I watched as he pulled forward and passed the grave. His complexion turned red in the haze of his backup lights through the open hatchback. I raised my hand and then waved my fingers, edging him closer to the hole. I held up my open palm and nodded when the tail end of his car hovered over the edge of the grave.

Kyle circles around the back of the car and rests his hands on his hips, staring down at the primitive grave. We waste no time grabbing bags and tossing them in. The slap of plastic weighed with something wet interrupts the sputter of his exhaust. I climb down into the pit as Kyle continues to empty the hatchback. As I maneuver the bags to make the surface as flat as possible, Kyle lets out a gagging sound. I pause and look up. Kyle covers his mouth and nose with the back of his hand, and I watch his stomach lurch. Once again, the reminder that there are perks to being dead. After I finish flattening the mound, we cover the hole. Kyle shakes his head, coughing to push the stench out of his nostrils and lungs as he uses the trowel to spread the earth over the strangers' parts. I follow with shovels of dirt.

We studied the site after we finished covering the bags. The fresh dirt rose a few feet above the ground. If someone wandered upon the mound, they would know something wasn't right. This was definitely a grave. There was little we could do about it besides hope. Tossing the tools into the back, we climbed into the car and headed back down the dirt road. I looked at the rearview. The burial site faded out of view as we bounced toward the main road. The sun split from behind the trees, killing what remained of yesterday. Kyle smiled at me as we turned onto the main road and headed back home.

## Chapter 11
## March 28th, 2024, 8:12 am.

I stumbled into my apartment and slammed the door behind me, waving my hand toward the far wall, cursing Kenny as I made my way to the couch. I locate the remote and collapse into the cushions. My forearm drapes my eyes as I reach out with the remote and turn on my television. What crackles to life on the screen isn't important. I just want something in the background to steady my nerves. Kyle dropped me at the front of my building and put his thumb and pinky on his face and shook his wrist. I nodded and listened to him drive away, wondering how he was digesting what we had just done. I am going to need to come clean with him. There was a preliminary plan. When I called after my nap, I'd suggest we meet for coffee to spin the wheels of normality. There I would confess, let Kyle completely into what had transpired the last few days. The first stranger that I Dracula'd in the basement. The body in the kitchen. There would be that *Ah-ha* moment that would explain the ease with which I dissected the third man in my tub. Then I would lay the rest on the table. Again, he would either run screaming, or… I don't know.

"I'm dead." That's how I would deliver it. Flat. Straight forward. Whether he thinks I am a raging lunatic does not allocate the level of respect that I owe him. He is my best friend. My only friend. The only person who I could trust with the disposal of a dead body, and he showed up. No questions asked. I need to believe he will take this information about my situation with grace. "Grace" isn't the right word, but you get my drift.

 A laugh track rolls in the background. A sitcom that I can't place now fills the space and lets the weight of my body sink into the couch. My forearm floats over my eyes. I should be able to smell the dirt and mud encrusted on my hoodie. I can't. Thank God, because I don't have the strength to throw up or change my clothes. I just want to sleep. Kyle has probably arrived home by now, collapsing wherever it is he sleeps. His mom and little sister are probably snoring in another room somewhere in the house. The echoes of their negligence reminding him that he doesn't matter. They are unaware of what he has done or where he has been, I am assuming. My cheeks should flush. They can't. These allocations I create are shallow and projective. I do not know what his family dynamic is outside of my fantasies. There has been very little discussion between us and that needs to change. We have both been discreet about the vulnerabilities of our lives. It doesn't make us less; it just makes us smart. Even the best of friends can find themselves engrossed in depressive, self-devastating foreplay. The finality of exposing ourselves to each other. Turning back isn't an option once you open that door.

 The laughter swirls into the hushing waves of water. Voices of strangers cheering contestants blur into waves crashing a speckled brown shore. I stand in front of a vast lake. In the distance, white-capped mountains defy gravity as they lean forward, hovering over the water. My peripherals fade into a deep blue vignette. I can't move my limbs. Waves crawl up the sand, gently touching my toes before retreating, as if forbidden to come closer. I scanned the glass surface of the lake. My eyelids are wide and stiff as my head twists from left to right, making a small ticking sound. Just beyond the focus of my gaze, a ripple forms, shattering the reflection of the clouds. The lake moans as something surfaces from beneath its mouth. Two more forms crest the water like fishing bobbers. Three humanoid silhouettes rise above the water, distorted within the dark shadows of the mountains. The peaks groan forward, casting a darkness that cuts against the shore, creating a chiaroscuro landscape. The three figures float forward, waist high in the murk. I still can't move my limbs. The anxiety pinches at my gut, threatening to expel any waste my corpse may be harboring.

The form on the far-right sways back and forth as the shadows of the lake move them nearer. The garbled vocalization that I can only describe as wet and choked, echoes across the void. *Murderer.* The word assaults my ears and worms its way into my decaying mind. *Murderer.* The other two chime in. My bowels release onto the sand. Its heat splashes against the back of my legs. The dead lungs in my chest thrust in and out, causing me to wheeze, wet and frantic.

*Murderer. Murderer. Murderer.*

Their faces break the shadows upon the shore. The couch man. Rotting flesh of familiar faces looking forward. The stranger in the kitchen. Mud slides down their visage. The floater. Grimy mouth, twisted and full of dirt, drops open in a mock laugh.

*Murderer. Murderer. Murderer.* They repeat as I try to scream.

I fell off my couch, throwing my arms out as I slammed to the floor. The coffee table screeches across the hardwood, and I roll onto my belly and stare at the wood pattern. I pinch my eyes shut and fold my hand under my chest to calm my heaving. My chest is completely still. With a pushup, I kneel on my living room floor and open my eyes. Being dead sucks.

\* \* \* \*

This may not make sense to you, but I took a shower to wake up and get clean. I am not sure if either of those things are possible, but I needed the familiarity of routine. I stood in the shower and looked over my body. My flesh looked a little grey, and the wounds on my chest and shoulders haven't healed. There was no feeling of water against my skin, putting me in a state of panic. Having this reality of emptiness is unbearable. I washed my body as I tried to settle myself down. Almost all my senses have eroded away, leaving me with the reality of nothing. There is no way I can explain this any clearer than the word nothing. Yet, it isn't a strong enough word. A vague descriptor at best. I finish my shower and step out into the mist, and stare at the frosted reflection above my sink. What occurs to me is a daunting realization.

*How long can I survive like this, really?*

Forget about the smell. My rotting carcass is becoming apparent to everyone around me. The paranoia I felt as I observed strangers, wondering if they knew. The overwhelming need to feel…anything. What will happen to us? Kyle and I? It won't surprise you to hear that things end badly for us. Well, for me.

I dress in loose clothing for no other reason than to hide my frail features. I have become gaunt. There is not much I can do for my facial features. The sunglasses I prop on my face suck my cheeks in more. They look like those oversized party glasses. I decided to leave them on, because despite their buggy appearance, they hide my eyes that have now discolored. Their light brown has turned into a milky white cloud that fades towards the pupil. There will be a time when even the miniature black dot will be nothing more than an off-colored spot. Lifeless and horrific. My outfit comprises a medium black t-shirt and a pair of loose blue jeans with holes in the knees. My emaciated kneecaps peeked out as I cross the room to my hallway closet to retrieve my jacket. I slip on my bright blue windbreaker and then check my reflection in the hallway mirror. *Dead AF.* I text Kyle.

*Coffee?*

*Give me ten.* He responds, and I make my way down the hall, checking over my shoulder for any spectators. I slip down the stairwell and out into the afternoon sun. I stare straight into its heart, letting its rays pelt my boney face. The darkness of my sunglass lenses chokes the star into a tight, radiant circle. With my hands securely stuffed into my front pockets, I cross the street and head towards Little Dutch Bistro. I would like to tell you I thought about what I would say to Kyle. How I would deliver the god-awful reality of my situation. For the sake of looking like I had a small part of my shit together, I would like to tell you those things. We both know I didn't. What I thought about was the Shuffler. Remember when I said I would come clean about my theory earlier? Since very little happened physically on my walk to the Bistro, let me tell you what I was thinking about on my way there.

We have discussed the Shuffler could be a *"something"*. A *"someone"*. I have always been under the impression, since I do not believe in a higher power, that the Shuffler indeed is a *"something"*. Not a spirit, or any of that weird shit. I know it presents a challenge in my perception and thoughts, now that I, myself, am something mystical, but I still hold firm that it isn't a spirit. This, *"something"*, is a control arm. Nothing more. A fabrication of the mind that we twist into reality. Giving birth to a living thing that now deals us random cards without prejudice or malice. It's like scratch-off tickets. You could win a little, a lot, or nothing at all. Except the price to play isn't monetary. It's your fucking life. So why do we play? Because it's in our nature to. Sure, you have some people out there that can go through life immune to the fixation. The addiction. The strong-willed people. They give themselves important titles like *mystic*, *healer*, and whatever other fancy name they can make up. They just are better than us. That's the reality. These individuals hold a wild card. The Joker. Or the Ace. When the *"something"* pulls a card, they flash their trump and walk the other way leaving the *"something"* to get substance elsewhere. The counter argument to this has always been to learn their ways. Especially from the higher ups. The better people. *Yogi, if it were indeed that easy, we would all be doing it.* So, there you have it. The Shuffler. The *"something"* that neither you nor I can escape because by nature we love to gamble, and I have lost big time.

Bright overhead LED lighting illuminates the front window to the Bistro. Strangers gather on couches and around huge round tables. I grit my teeth as they sip from steaming cups. I mentally prepare myself to purchase a beverage I cannot smell or taste. Then, I will sit next to my best friend, whom I spent hump day with burying a stranger, and confess that I am dead. The t-shaped advertisement on the sidewalk boasts the Thursday special. Matcha. I turned my nose up. Even though I was dead, I wouldn't drink that shit. The chorus melody from "Thunder only happens when it's raining" climbs from my bowels as I look at the bright orange letters spelling Thursday. The timing of the irony is perfect. Thor and Thursday. Jupiter. All dealing with thunder and lightning. Well played, Shuffler.

The door jingles when I walk in. The little bells sound louder today as a few people look over at me and then return to their conversations. I scanned the room and spot Kyle sitting at our usual table. I nod and make my way to the counter.

"Would you like to try out the matcha special today?" I don't read the new kid's nametag, ignoring his question.

"I'll take a *Cinnamon Spice and Vanilla is Nice,* please. Mug." I say, staring up at the menu on the back wall.

I leave a two-dollar tip on the counter and make my way to our table. Kyle slumps in his chair, lazily sipping from his mug.

"Long night." He smiles from behind his rim. "And what's up with the shades, Goose?"

I give him a confused look as I fall into my seat. He waves me off. Later, I would reflect on my ignorance concerning pop culture films. I sip from my cup and let the liquid slide down my throat. The muscles in my throat haven't worked for days and I am pretty sure I still have some Lo Mein lodged in there.

"I just wanted to say thanks for-" Kyle cuts me off with a raised palm.

"No need, man." He slurps and smacks his lips.

*I hate it when he does that.*

"Rather not talk about that for a bit. I am still digesting it all."

With a nod, he takes another slurp and shuffles his weight and gives me a toothy smile. I can't blame him. What we did was a lot for anyone to take in. For me, this has all been one huge, demented dream. I would pinch myself to see if I was dreaming, if I could feel it. My eyes focus behind the black shields, and I grip my mug tighter, trying to strangle heat into my palm. Something to show that I am alive. At some point, I need to give up on it.

"You ever hear of DBT?" I ask, adjusting my shades.

Kyle gives me an odd look and shuffles upright in his seat. "Can't say I have, bro."

I pretend to clear my throat and set my mug on the arm of my chair. "It's called Dialectical Behavior Therapy. Saw it on a late-night show."

Kyle pulls the corners of his mouth down and tilts his head. "Sounds fucking boring." He raises his eyebrows and takes another sip.

I ignore the comment and continue. "It's meant to force you to confront the reality of reality."

Kyle just stares at me, allowing me to continue.

"It keeps pain from turning into suffering. Well, in theory." I add.

"You watch way too much late-night television, my friend," he chimes in and then leans forward, signaling me to get to the point before his attention span disintegrates.

"I need to accept reality for what it really is." Like Dr. Frankenstein, my body tries to bring the worm of anxiety back to life in my stomach.

A flat expression forms on Kyle's face. "Is this about last night, Thane?" The look of terror on his face pulls the color from his cheeks and his shoulders tighten.

I held up my hand and let out a chuckle. "No," I smile. Kyle relaxes in his chair and lets out a nervous laugh. He sips from his mug and clamps his eyes shut. When he looks back up at me, his eyes are smiling.

"You almost scared the shit out of me, dude." He tilts the mug and rocks it up and down. "So, what's this all about, then?"

I tighten my grip around my mug and look him dead in the eyes. *No pun intended.* When the words form in my rotting vocal chords and gargle forward, I watch his face contort.

"I'm turning into a zombie." I sputter as I stare at him from behind my tinted glasses. Kyle's wrist goes slack. His mug tilts and coffee splashes on the floor next to his foot.

"You're fucking doing what?" He raises his voice, drawing the attention of a couple of tables nearby. They look back and forth between us. The man's cup hovers below his bottom lip. The woman coughs and they return to their conversation. I straighten my posture and square my shoulders. I pull down my glasses and set them on the table.

"I'm dead." I whisper.

\* \* \* \*

His eyes shift back and forth in micro movements. I try to remain composed as I wait for a crazy outburst. It never comes. Kyle's pupils focus in and out as he studies my face. I wait. I have all the time in the world. He needs time to digest what I just laid on him. Kyle places his cup on the table and leans back in his seat, folding his fingers together. When he breaks the silence, it starts with a deep breath and a pause. He pursed his lips, squinting his eyes. The upper lip rises, showing his top teeth, and Kyle grins and says,

"Whatever all this is," he separates his hands, waving one in the air before refolding them and letting them fall onto his chest. "We can skip the weird shit. I am not in the mood."

"I'm dead, Kyle, and have been for quite a few days now." I say this in a serious tone, and Kyle tests it again with a smirk. When I don't return the sentiment, his smile fades as he tightens his fingers together. His lips straighten into a thin line.

"Are you mental?" He says sharply.

I should be offended, but I'm not. I understand. How often does your best friend say something like this? There is also nothing to relate this experience to. I can't think of anything that would compete or equate to talking to a dead guy. Ghosts don't count because they are not real. Kyle stares at me as he reaches for his coffee. His pupils tighten into specks like the head of a pin. I put my glasses back on to escape his gaze as he pulls his mug back with him in the chair.

"I don't know if you have lost your fucking mind since last night, bro, but whatever this is all about, I ain't having it." He sips from his mug and purses his lips with a disappointed scowl.

"I get it," He continues. "What happened was crazy, but we need to keep our wits, man." I nodded my head, so he stopped talking.

"I'm not crazy, Kyle. This is serious." I lean forward and pull my jacket down around my shoulders. Kyle looks around the room and then gives me an expression that screams *stop it*. I pulled the edge of my T-shirt down to show him the wounds. Kyle stares at my bare chest. As I wait for a response, the air in the room grows thick. Kyle just stares in bewilderment.

"They won't heal." I say.

Kyle shakes his head. "What won't heal?" He scans the room again to see if anyone is watching us.

"The wounds." I tuck my chin in and tilt my head. My chest is bare. I pull the shirt aside more. They are gone.

Kyle sets his cup down and leans closer to me. "Maybe we should go, man." His voice sounds sad now. His voice carries the tone reserved for a child.

I pull the other side of my shirt down and inspect my chest and shoulders. There are no wounds. You would expect me to lose my mind, but I don't. The Shuffler, for once, played in my favor. Let me explain. As Kyle chattered away, I looked around the room. No one was paying the slightest attention to us. How could that be? Even the couple that gawked at us prior sipped their matcha and flirted back and forth without batting an eye at the conversation taking place right next to them. A dead dude, showing his best friend his rotting flesh, that now isn't even there. Why before and not now? This conversation was much more exciting. That's when I knew. That is when it fell into place. Everyone here knew. Somehow, they were in on all this. Why and how I didn't know, and still don't, but let me say this. I don't care how or why. My concern was that they did, and Kyle, for whatever reason, was now with them. The concern on his face was nothing more than a game.

\* \* \* \*

We sat in silence for quite some time. A few of the surrounding tables had become abandoned, leaving their mugs and paper cups behind. The couple at the table closest to us that had gawked gave me a side eyed glance before leaving. I wanted to feel a flush, just so I could have something familiar. I needed it. Craved it. When Kyle finished his coffee, he ran his finger over the rim and stared into space. He cleared his throat and, setting his mug down, pushed his chair back and stood above me across the table.

"I'm going for another coffee. Want another?" He asked. His voice was soft. There was a bit of sorrow that leaked behind the edges of the words. No, not sorrow. Pity. I shook my head. Kyle took his mug and went to stand in line for a refill. I took the moment for myself. As I walked to the bathroom, keeping my eyes forward, there was an urge to look back at Kyle. As if it were the last time I would see what remained of my best friend. The real Kyle. There was a possibility that, although Kyle knew things about the undead, he wasn't necessarily against me. Or lying. This could be an act. Kyle playing dumb, hoping that all this crazy shit would filter through to reality. A normality that resembled us before I became dead. Maybe. I entered the bathroom and approached the sink, keeping my eyes on my feet. I placed my open palms against the counter and closed my eyes. My wounds, somehow, some way, have disappeared. I search for fear. That familiar feeling of losing control. The trigger of human responses before all of this had started. When I was still…alive. It isn't there. As my eyelids squeeze together, I search my decaying brain. If there is anything left of my senses, it needs to comfort me. But I feel nothing. I open my eyes. The corpse in the mirror stares back at me in disgust. His lips press into a thin line. My eyes wander to his chest. He pulls the black t-shirt aside and lets me see the graying flesh of his collar bone.

*More?* He mocks.

"Yes." I say, watching as he pulls the fabric down, exposing his bare chest. No wounds.

I wait for the little wiggle of anxiety to form in the pit of my stomach. It doesn't. The last remaining sense faded and gone. I want to feel loss, but it doesn't form. Sorrow is something that the living can experience. I now realize I am one hundred percent dead. The conversation I will now have with Kyle needs to be deliberate. I need to know what he knows. I pull the edge of my shirt down and check for the wounds. As I run my hand over my bare chest, I smile.

*Am I going mad? Have I lost my mind somewhere between sleep and reality? But isn't sleeping reality? Thoughts mix with emotions and responses to physical stimuli. I think so. Somewhere, in the everyday motion of being awake and sleeping,*

*I died. And now, I have nothing. Except what's left of my mind.*

\* \* \* \*

Kyle sits in his chair sipping his coffee. The steam from his mug bends his facial features. His hand slightly shakes. Envy would be a godsend right now. Anything to pull me back to the living. My cup sits empty where I left it, and I sit down and try to sink into the seat. Kyle cups his mug in his hands and overlaps his fingers. He is trying to hide the trembling.

"I'm not crazy." The words flow out naturally. As a fact.

Kyle stares at the tabletop, his fingertips turning white as he squeezes the mug. "Thane, I'm not saying-" He closes his eyes when I interrupt him.

"Yes, you are. Or at least you're thinking it." I say.

As visions of the three strangers flash in my mind, the chorus of "*Psycho Killer*" by Talking Heads plays in a loop. But I can't run away and neither can Kyle. We have to work this out. He must understand that I am not some lunatic. After all, wasn't it he who helped me bury the floater? If I am crazy, then he is holding up the rear.

"I just think that maybe what we did has done something to you." His voice pulls me back to reality. I hear what he says echo in a thumping delay throughout my body.

"I don't think it has." I respond.

Kyle gives me a hard look and grips his mug tighter. It looks as if it could crumble in his hands at any moment.

"Thane." He pauses as he investigates the rising steam of his coffee mug. "You think you're a zombie, dude."

I wait because I know there's more that he wants to say, and I need to hear everything before I speak my piece. What I know to be the truth.

"You showed me wounds that aren't there, man." Kyle sets his coffee on the table and folds his hands in his lap. "You need help, Thane." His voice held concern. The tone was pleading, not demanding. I put my hand to my dead chest. The lack of a heartbeat reminds me of why this is so true to me, but it is hard for Kyle to understand. How could I expect him to? I still struggle with my situation. I chose my next words wisely.

"You ok?" I try to keep my facial reaction neutral. Kyle nods his head, and I notice his shoulders relax.

"Maybe you're right." I say flatly. "Maybe I could talk to someone."

Kyle straightens in his seat. The corners of his mouth tremble as he forces a smile. He still has something he is not telling me.

"Good." He reaches for his coffee.

I watch him sip from his mug and scan the room. Then it comes. He was trying to hold back. He spills it forward. Self-preservation disguised as a nonchalant mention.

"You won't mention last night, right?" He keeps his eyes on his beverage, and I grit my teeth. The absence of anger frustrates me. I want to rip his head off. Toss it into the garbage can on my way out the door. But I felt nothing. No betrayal. No anger. Not even sorrow.

"Not a word." I smile and snatch my mug from the table.

"Looks like I need another coffee." My chair slides back and I stand, focusing my eyes on the top of Kyle's skull. "I'll call my doctor in the morning." I say with the most honest voice I can muster. "Promise." I add.

Kyle looks at me. The worry in his eyes is for his situation, not me, even though I want to think otherwise. He is an accomplice. Kyle watched as I dismantled that man. He was there digging the hole. The evidence is on his family's property. Again, I can't blame him. I need him more than he realizes. He is the only thing alive in this world. My world. Did he feel remorse when he found out how I ended up? Under my bed, with a hole in my chest. I am sure a sense of relief followed. I would be a liar if I said I would have felt differently had the roles had been reversed.

When I left the cafe that night, I had to give Kyle some space. I assured him I would never speak a word about that night. I kept my promise. The sad reality, and I stress the word reality, Kyle didn't keep his promise. He didn't stay in my life. He left when I needed him most. I'm getting ahead of the story again. Let me slow down and explain how this night ended.

## Chapter 12
## March 28th, 2024, 5:12 pm.

I spent the afternoon walking around town. It seemed better to me than staring at the walls of my apartment. I stayed away from people and kept to the more unpopular streets. I kept my eyes on the ground, watching cars out of my peripheral. The stranger's eyes burned through the glass as they gawked at the dead guy strolling around town. Some of them for sure knew, slowing their cars slightly as they approached from behind. I could hear the rotation of their tires slow, taking in the spectacle like I was some weird animal in a safari exhibit.

*Look at the corpus mortuum. Such a unique species. It cannot feel. No sense of emotion or sensory impulses. No, no, don't get close. They bite, and it doesn't want your snacks. It only eats brains.*

The revving sound of an engine as they pick up speed in passing. All occupants looking straight forward so they don't look guilty. The undead shake their heads. The disappointment in one of their own not blending in well enough.

I go to the public track and sit on the bleachers. A different woman jogs the dirt circle, and I pretend not to notice how uncomfortable she is with me being there. She picks up the pace when she passes around my side of the track, and I can't help but feel sorry for her. The stress in simple everyday activities must be unbearable. The effects and consequences of exposure to something heinous. I watch the ground five feet below and listen to her steps patter against the gravel. Louder, then fading as she makes her way to the outer perimeter of the track. A rabbit running in circles trying to extend its life on this rock. Fighting for a few more years of madness. Insanity by definition. All the while, fearing a stranger sitting alone, separated by several feet of aluminum seats and a chain linked fence. As you know, I will expire. Under a bed. That's the term I will use because I am already dead, but at that moment, on the bleachers, I question it. There was a nagging suspicion that I may end up roaming the earth forever. Unlike the rabbit on the track, I don't have to do anything to improve my chances of remaining here. To add time to my existence. My body already succumbed to it. My mind and being, unfortunately, did not. Fear isn't something I could feel, but there was a sense of something like it. The nag, as I described it, ate at me, driving me insane. It was like fear in the sense that I felt out of control. There was nothing I could do about my situation but exist in it.

When I looked up from my perch, I was alone. Somehow, within my thoughts, the stranger had left the track. The echoes of her feet stayed behind, masking her escape. The sun was dropping behind the trees, and I pulled out my cell phone. Seven o'clock. As I made my way down the steps, I contemplated remaining out all night, just to see if I could feel the cold. Of course I can't, but I will tell you, at this point in the story, I was desperate for any semblance of normality.

**March 28th, 2024, 8:30 pm.**

The silhouette sitting at the table almost escaped detection in the dim lighting of my kitchen. I stood completely still, focusing on the stark outer lines of its form. The contrast between the black void of its body and the dim lighting of the background created illusions. The form seemed to pulsate and grow, filling the space. I balled my fist and dug them into my eyes, pressing inward, hoping to feel pain. The room ebbed as I refocused on the stranger. Is he dead? Another unknown corpse I would have to dispose of. I couldn't do this again. My breaking point, which to be fair, I wasn't sure existed anymore, felt imminent. As I backed up, I focused my rotting orbs on the void. It was so still that I questioned its validity. I reached my hand out when my back bumped against the door, and I flicked the light switch. The room was empty. The smallest tinge of anxiety tried so hard to birth itself, fading into the pit of my decomposing entrails. I jostled the switch on and off, strobing the room. The void crept closer and closer, like the ending scene in a classic horror film standoff. I reached down and squeezed the phone resting in my pocket. I needed to call Kyle. When I flicked the light on for the last time, its yellow fluorescence stabbed my eyes. The stillness was uncomfortable. Heavier than the imaginary void at the table. There was a small part of me that wouldn't have minded the stranger being real. A morbid visitor to occupy the loneliness. I made my way to the living room and turned on my lights. I needed to illuminate my world. Clear my mind. I turned on the television, pressing the volume knob hard. Kathleen predicted rain, swooping her hand over a green screen map of our county. Her black blouse and matching dress pants made her look like she was attending a funeral. There was a loud bang against the wall, and I took the volume down a few notches.

"Sorry, Kenny!" I yelled across the room.

A solitary knock echoed through my apartment, accepting the apology, and I set the remote down and headed back to the kitchen. I would have loved to have made coffee, but now it seems fruitless. Almost ignorant. The ritual that used to provide comfort now leaves me with little more than sadness. So, I resigned to sit at the table and try to come up with a plan to fix my situation. What could I possibly do at this point? Kyle, the only person who could have helped me, now, I am sure, thinks I am batshit crazy. I am still convinced he won't go to the police. After all, he would hang himself. He might be crazy for helping me, but he isn't stupid. I would feel guilty about it if I could, but I can't feel anything anymore. My fingers tap the tabletop, a familiar rhythm that takes me a second to recognize. My brain recalls the first line of "Seven Nation Army" by The White Stripes, pulling forward the lyrics just in time for the next phrase. I picture the silhouettes of Jack and Meg White with sharp frames of red climbing behind them. I close my eyes and watch the music video in high def; the audio melding into Dolby

Surround that echoes through my entire body. As the song peters out, I realize I am exhausted. I think. Or maybe overwhelmed. It has been so long since I have felt anything that I can't remember how to feel. These responses are now ghosts of my dying nervous system.

\* \* \* \*

My bed is the end of the world. The darkness swirls. White chalk paint cast shadows from their dunes across the vast desert of my ceiling. Time seems endless now. Is this how the Shuffler feels it? Does it ebb from moment to moment, blending on and on into infinity? Probably. We share that now. As one headspace. Understanding the darkness of things. The Shuffler knows my end. If there is one. Or, if I am unlucky, this will go on forever. My phone sat on the nightstand next to my broken alarm clock, and I thought about what Kyle must have been doing. Was he lying in bed, staring at his ceiling? Wondering if his crazy ass friend has indeed lost his mind? I wanted to call him, but I knew better. Even if he answered, I would not try to convince him I am undead. I am not changing any minds. He had made that clear earlier in the cafe. What I needed to do was convince him I would not become a liability. That helping me wasn't a risk.

I close my eyes and attempt to relax. I can still feel the desert above my head swirling. There is a pulsing that starts. Slow at first. It builds into a thumping that pounds off the inner walls of my skull, ringing in my ears like a ball peen hammer against steel. When I open my eyes, the sound fades into a thousand bees. It erupts from the left side of my head, and I crank my neck. The broken alarm clock illuminates when the thousand bees return, lighting up my cell phone. I realized then that somehow, someway; I slept. Even if briefly, I slept. There is hope, after all. I would have yelled hallelujah, but that isn't my style. Some would say that maybe it was the reason for the problem and the cause of my situation. My legs thump to the floor as I twist my body upright and look down at my phone screen. Kyle's contact hovers above his number and I rub my right eye with the back of my hand as I pick up the phone and press the button. Kyle's voice sounds odd. There is an overbearing tone of joy that sounds processed. Manufactured.

"How's it going, man?" He says.

"Oh," I answer, trying to keep my tone neutral, in case I am exaggerating my worry. I'm not.

There is a heavy silence that exposes the space between our phones. I can hear his breath. Short and ragged, laced with concern. *What have you done, Kyle?*

"We should do coffee." He says flatly.

I want to say no, but if we don't, I won't hear the bad news that I know sits on the tip of his tongue.

"Yeah." I answer.

More silence.

"Okay, then!" He says. Falsetto pulls his voice up, making him sound like a child. Another stretch of silence that presses on my chest. If I could breathe, I would hold it.

"We need to talk, huh?" I say.

Long silence.

"Yeah, we do." Kyle says.

\* \* \* \*

I enter the Bistro and immediately approach the counter. I am too riled up to pay attention to who is working at the front counter. Without making eye contact, I dropped a five-dollar bill on the counter and ordered my *Cinnamon Spice and Vanilla is Nice*. There is a voice that takes the order and then repeats it back like a parrot. I still won't make eye contact, nor do I look over toward our meeting place. I know he is there, waiting for me with whatever this *news* is. As I leave the change and make my way toward the table, I scan the room. Anywhere but where Kyle is sitting. Strangers sip from paper cups and colored mugs with the Bistro logo. I can't make out what they're saying. A tall gentleman wearing tight black jeans and a bright red Adidas windbreaker looks up at me and nods as if we know each other. We don't. It's when I avert my attention that my eyes finally contact Kyle. He smiles at me, leaning back in his seat with his usual coffee. The smile differs from usual, which stirs a tickle in the pit of my stomach. I pull my seat and settle in, placing my mug toward the edge of the table. It gives me something to play with. If needed, something that could occupy my mind. Something I could throw. The intrusive thought wins for a moment and I push it back where it belongs. No matter what Kyle has to say, I could never do that. The thought of assaulting my best friend makes me wish I could feel shame. I pretend to take a deep breath and watch the brown liquid swirl in my cup. To have the comfort of taste and smell would be wonderful right now. The lack of anxiety was a blessing, but whatever took its place had created a hole. A rotting crevice. A void where I am stuck feeling, but not feeling. Just nothing and then again, everything. Kyle slurped his coffee, smacked his lips, and plastered on that fake smile again.

"What's going on?" I say, putting the conversation in motion.

Kyle pinches his bottom lip between his thumb and forefinger and looks toward the rug. I want to scream. He just sits there, staring at the floor. Only when his hand trembles as he pulls it away from his mouth do I understand the news is foul.

"I have to leave." He says. His voice is rough and choked. The edges of his eyes look wet, and I realize he is crying.

"What are you talking about?" I ask.

Kyle focuses hard on his mug, and he tilts his head awkwardly. The corners of his mouth quiver and he grips his mug tight.

"We can't hang anymore, man." Our eyes connect. "They are moving me to another wing." There is a vacant look in his eyes, like he is trying to fight something he has no control over.

"Another wing. What are you talking about?" The lack of emotion makes my voice sound uninterested, and Kyle's face flattens like he is looking at a stranger.

"I don't have a choice, Thane." He answers. His voice now harbors anxiety.

"We always have choices, dude." I retort. I want to sound angry and usually that emotion is easy to fake. At that moment, I failed in the delivery of my words epically.

"Listen, Thane." He held up his hand and I cut him off.

"Is this about," I scan the room and lower my voice and lean in, resting my elbows on the table. "The body?"

Kyle stares at me wide eyed. The confusion on his face fools me for a second, and then he adds, "What? What are you talking about, dude?" While squinting his eyes.

"You know exactly what the fuck I am talking about, Kyle!" I raise my voice and stand up. A few people look over at us and I shoot them a *mind your own business* look.

A stranger comes from somewhere across the room. He is slender, with an athletic build, and looks strong for his age. I think I recognized him, but I am not sure. He approaches us, extending his hands out, palms up.

"You ok, man?" He says calmly, as if he is trying to quell an uncontrollable force. I turn my attention to Kyle, only to realize the guy is referring to me. I scoff at him and turn my attention back to Kyle.

"So, what, you're just gonna skip town? Fuck me, right?" I lean palms down on the table. The man takes a few steps closer, and I spin around.

"You need to leave," he says, pointing his index finger.

I freeze. "Don't tell me what I *need* to do!" I look at Kyle, who has now stood up and backed away. "Get away from me!" I point at the stranger and circle the side of the table as I scan the room for a clear path to the exit. He takes a step forward and I fake to the left, and he falls for it. I swing to the right and jolt past the stranger and close my eyes as I rush for the door.

My mind feels heavy as I break through the door and head down the street. The stranger's feet slap against the street behind me. He follows me to the end of the street and then gives up. When I reach my apartment complex, I slam the door behind me and take the stairs a few at a time. I reach my apartment and fumble to open the door. When I slam it behind me, I run to the living room and grab my lounge chair. With inhuman strength, I lift it and carry it, propping it up against the door making a barricade. I lock the knob and step back. Kenny pounds on the wall and I cover my ears.

"I'm trying to watch my show, ya son of a bitch!" his voice echoes through my apartment. It slithers through the air, wet and dead. *He's a zombie too now.* I ran to my bedroom and shut the door. The dark room ebbs, expanding into a huge void. I curl up at the foot of my bed and cover my head with my forearms. I close my eyes and scream.

* * * *

It was a few days later when the police barged into my apartment. Their voices boomed from behind my door, yelling my name over and over. They kicked the door in and rushed across my living room to my bedroom door. I am sure the warden sent them. Folded her arms across her chest and saying *I never liked that fucking kid, horrible patient. Can't fix that mess.* Kenny probably craned his neck from behind his door, wide eyed, feigning shock. I'll piss off my landlord with the broken door, and I'll lose part of my security deposit, but I don't care. It's not like I'm going to get that back. Wait until he sees the stain under the bed from my chest. The liquid from my demolished heart. The ichor is tainting the hardwood. I had slid under my bed to hide. To cover the wound Kyle had made. The hole. The officer's feet thumped across my floor. My dead heart beats to life, matching the random steps. Slowing as my eyes clouded over. I was dying. Actually dying. I can't tell you how this was possible. Returning to the land of the living. Because I was already dead. But it happened. It happened the minute I realized I would go back there. Back to residential care. Back to the state hospital.

Where am I now? I am not sure anymore. Probably the same place Thelma, Allison, and Kieth wound up. I hope. Someday. As I lay there gripping the hole in my chest, my heart shattered and broken, I thought about my alarm clock and what might have happened to it. Would they just toss it in the garbage? It doesn't belong there. It's an icon. A special item reminding us of a place in an infinite time. People really wanted that model in the 80s. It was the Rolex of alarm clocks. It doesn't deserve to be tossed aside and forgotten like most everything else in this world. Someone should put it in a museum, so people can remember a time when things were fun and pure. Not rotten and dead. Like now. I didn't think about Thelma. Her thin body, frail in her casket. I didn't think about *Cinnamon Spice and Vanilla is Nice*. Nor were there any thoughts about the couch man, the kid, or the floater. I didn't see Allison dragging her mangled form across the road toward Kieth. The squirrel's tail, twitching above its body. Its eyes staring into oblivion. The rock above my head, waiting to come down and put an end to it all. I just closed my eyes and let the rock fall.

## Chapter 13:
## April 9th, 2021, 3:00 p.m.
### Kyle

I met Thane Mortimer during intake, as I do most patients. I will admit that our relationship may have been different if I hadn't taken the afternoon shift that day. One of the floor nurses called off, and my cell phone rang while I was heating my dinner in the microwave. I had queued up episode six of True Crime with Maury, while I watched my bowl of chicken noodle soup spin behind the dirty glass. As soon as the chime echoed across the room, I knew it was work. Sometimes, I wish I never answered that day. It hurts me to think that maybe my life would have been better if I had met Thane under different circumstances. The connection formed between a patient and a medical professional is relative to that first impression. This is true on both sides. We are, after all, humans. If a staff member comes across as too bold or pushy, that can set the patient into fight-or-flight mode and connect a negative emotion that ties to that staff member. It doesn't matter the reason. Maybe the nurse or doctor has had a terrible day, or didn't sleep well the night before. The why doesn't matter. It is our job to minimize the occurrence, and we always don't quite hit the mark. I know I certainly failed in that aspect with Thane.

I clocked in and checked with the front desk. Sheryl Clemmens tapped away on the keyboard, focusing on the monitor like her life depended on it. An oversized bottle of water sat next to a mug of coffee.

"How's it going, Sheryl?" I leaned on the counter and stared down at the blond bun that bobbed on top of her head. A strong floral smell bit my nostrils, and I leaned back a few inches, hoping it would make a difference. Nope. She looked up from under her eyebrows and scoffed with a crooked smile.

"Same shit, different day. You in for Jen?"

I nodded and turned toward the large plate glass that separated the nursing station from the main floor. Patients sat on couches and at tables playing cards or staring off into a world that none of us could see. I felt sorrow and envy. There is shame in that thought process. We don't know what they witness in that other space. What Hell. I pretend to think the opposite. That they are in a tranquil place, away from all of this. The confines of a confine.

"You are a lucky man tonight." Sheryl stops tapping and tosses a green intake folder onto the counter. "You get Jen's intake." She says, smiling wickedly before continuing to peck. "He's a repeater." She adds, grabbing her water barrel, shoving the tip of the fat plastic straw in her mouth and taking the smallest of sips. I pull the folder forward and flip open the cover. Thane Mortimer. A fifty-year old male. Five foot six, Caucasian. I turn my attention to the intake room that sits next to the main floor. The small, wired glass window gives me a clear shot at the white wall of the eight by twelve-foot room. On a cot, in the far corner, sits Thane. I close the folder and bounce it off the counter.

"Anything I need to know before I intake?"

Sheryl stops tapping and blows air up at her bangs. "Thane is a gentle soul. Never any trouble, really." She looks at his folder and pauses. When she looks up at me again, there's sadness there. I know that look and I know that feeling. Thane is a repeater. Repeater sometimes feels like a softer word for the phrase *we couldn't help*.

"Take a moment with the file." Her eyes become serious. "He has a very unique situation. It's why we chose Jen to intake him again, no offense."

"None taken." I assert. A fake smile splits my face.

"I asked them to call you first." She smiles in a way that I believe her. "So, take a moment with the file before you go in." She nods. "He is fine right now. We have his favorite show on." She goes back to pecking and micro-sipping, and I slide the folder off the counter and head for the break room. As I walk, I stare at the folder.

*A unique situation.*

That is what she had said. I have seen quite a few unique situations during my time at Commons, but the way she said it made me think it was over my head. But not over Jen's? Yeah, I am jealous of the favoritism here. But really, let's be fair. It isn't favoritism. Jen is just a damn good nurse. Like Fred. A cut above the rest of us. That is all it is. I enter the break room and cross the room to the far end table. A few other nurses occupy tables near the door. They are chatting and eating lunch, or maybe dinner, and I let out a grumble, remembering the meal I left in the microwave. The vending machine offers garbage I shouldn't eat, and I chose as wisely as possible. I squeeze the granola bar in my hand and dispense a bottle of water. I settle down in the hard plastic chair and flip Thane Mortimer's folder open.

\* \* \* \*

The first thing that caught my attention was the sharpness of his eyes. The fact is the public has a twisted representation of what our patients look like. Hollywood, for the sake of storytelling and profits, has painted these afflictions with a certain stigma. There is a look adopted by the public, either through entertainment or worst-case scenario reporting. Manic movements and wild stares, coupled with erratic language and behavior. Although this is true, it isn't always the case. The latter is not the common viewpoint of the public. Or at least what they are spoon-fed. Thane smiles in the photo. His black straggly hair covers his ears, and his eyes peek out from under his bangs, smiling at the camera. He looks young for a fifty-year-old. There are a few other photos in the case file. Most look like the top photo, a few have him sporting a bright blue windbreaker, zipped up tight under his chin. Except for his wild hair, he looks clean. Short stubble speckles his chin, brightening the pink of his lips. He looks, for all intents and purposes…happy. There was one photo, shuffled in the middle of the stack, that showed a slight variation to the rest. The variation was in the eyes. In the still, Thane seems to be distracted, looking past the camera. His eyes are wide and glossed. There is a sense of emptiness in them that structures his face in such a way that you could mistake him for someone else if you didn't have the other photos for reference. His lips still have a bright pink hue, the gleam of his white teeth poke through his slight pout. The hair, same. The bright blue windbreaker zipped tight to his chin. Speckled black scruff lined his jaw, the muscles in his jaw slack as if he were relaxed. But those eyes. He was somewhere else then. Somewhere beyond the room. Beyond the camera.

When I came to the diagnosis, and its explanation, I let out an audible gasp. One of the other staff members looked up from their meal and I cleared my throat. "Sorry," I said. The apology had a nervous delivery, and I turned my attention back to the form, with heat burning my cheeks.

Thane suffered from Cotard's syndrome. Also known as Cotard's delusion or walking corpse syndrome. A few unique aspects characterize this rare mental disorder. The afflicted feel they have died or are dead. Sometimes they think they are immortal, and that they are non-existent. Delusions about death sometimes accompany the syndrome, leading to depression and paranoia. In the case of Mr. Mortimer, he believes others may be dead as well and that they are lying or hiding it. He had expressed this through some of his transcripts, at least the ones I had thumbed through. The root cause of Cotard's is unknown, but can range from severe depression, bipolar disorders, tumors, to dementia. The list is vast, but there is one that strikes a stake through my heart. It is what they assume is the root cause attributing to Thane's diagnosis. Traumatic brain injury. When I flip through the pages, I have to stop and wipe my eyes several times. I bow my head, tucking my chin into my chest so the other staff members can't see the tears that speckle his paperwork.

Thane was six years old when his mother and father had died. The information pertaining to Kieth and Allison Mortimer was privileged, and I had to accept that they were good people. That's the narrative written and I have no reason to believe otherwise. This transcript also omits the accident's cause, and it abbreviates the scene's details. What is clear is that Kieth had died on impact. Allison was alive for a few hours. They found her near her husband's body. The impact of the crash threw her twenty feet from the vehicle, and in shock, she dragged herself to Kieth. Thane, buckled in the back car seat, had survived. When the fire department and ambulance had arrived, they reported Thane was staring blankly at his parents' bodies. Reports show that while the firefighter cut the car door, Thane sat calm and unresponsive. It was only when the man had reached in to take him from the wreck did the child begin to scream. The reports state he clawed at the firemen's mask, pointing to his parents and howling incoherently before convulsing into a seizure. A medical examination showed severe brain trauma. The type of TBI, or traumatic brain injury, is called a closed brain injury. Damage occurs without penetrating the skull. The brain hits the walls of the skull without breaking it, hence the term "closed brain." A large number of patients have a steep decline in their daily lives. Some die within a few years of the TBI diagnosis. Thane was in the higher percentile and was progressing with therapy and a home nurse. The state placed him with his grandmother. His folder contains little information about her beyond her name, Thelma, her widowed status, and her identity as Thane's maternal grandmother. Thane was in his late teens when he had his first inpatient care. From the report, which wasn't exactly thorough, Thane had relapsed and pulled forth memories of seeing his parents die. There was also a file in the report about a dying squirrel on the side of the road by his house. A car hit it, and Thane used a rock to euthanize it. He described its twitching tail as his mother telling him to run away. Thane recalls the incident happening before his parents demise. Like an omen. The report filled out by the child services department dated the incident occurring several years after the crash. That session was also the first instance where Thane had confessed that he had negative destructive thoughts. Self-harm and depressive states in which he would look in the mirror and see a dead version of himself staring back. The following month was his first month in the residential wing. The intake date puts him at nineteen. He was an adult, but a young adult. From then on, there is a back-and-forth documentation between at-home care and residential stays, some lasting up to four months. I closed the folder and twisted the cap off my water bottle and gulped it down. The other staff members had left the room, and the silence screamed in my ears like a loud static buzz. I tucked the folder under my armpit and tossed my empty water bottle in the trash and went to the nurse's station. Sheryl texts on her phone when I approach, and she holds up one finger. I wait, watching as she giggles and then rolls her eyes, tossing the phone on the desk, and then smiling up at me.

"You ready?" She hovers her finger over the lock button to the main door.

"As ready as I can ever be." I smile back, hoping my eyes haven't given away that I have bawled my eyes out for the last fifteen minutes.

Sheryl grins and presses the button. A buzzing sound pinches my ears, turning heads in the main room to the door. I hear the click and swing the door open and shut it quickly behind me, keeping my eyes on the patients that have remained completely still. Most of them have feigned interest right after the buzz, going back to their puzzles, crafts, and television shows. I turn to my right and walk up to the intake room and peek in through the tiny window. Thane lay on the bed watching the television that is suspended in the upper right corner of the room. He is a spitting image of his last photo. When I grip the door handle, he turns his head and sits up on the bed. I enter the room, painting on a big smile.

"Thane Mortimer?" I approached the end of the bed, keeping his file tucked under my arm.

Thane rotates his eyes, pressing them hard against the corners of their sockets. A wide grin splits his face as he tucks his arms under the thin hospital blanket. "You watch The Weather Channel?" His voice is low and serious.

I nodded.

"You like Kathleen Kempt?" he widens his grin.